The Herb for Happiness

The Duke caught [...]

"I want to loo[...]
you are not a fign[...]

"Why should I[...]

"It is almost i[...] so young to know so many things that are not granted to other people."

Selma smiled and as if she had answered, he said:

"You have already lived a thousand lives as a Healer, a Doctor, or—a Witch!"

"You make it sound very exciting." Selma smiled. "When you return home, you might write a book."

"With you as the heroine?" the Duke enquired. "Who would be the hero?"

For one moment her eyes met his.

It was impossible for either of them to look away...

A Camfield Novel of Love
by Barbara Cartland

Camfield Place,
Hatfield
Hertfordshire,
England

Dearest Reader,

Camfield Novels of Love mark a very exciting era of my books with Jove. They have already published nearly two hundred of my titles since they became my first publisher in America, and now all my original paperback romances in the future will be published exclusively by them.

As you already know, Camfield Place in Hertfordshire is my home, which originally existed in 1275, but was rebuilt in 1867 by the grandfather of Beatrix Potter.

It was here in this lovely house, with the best view in the county, that she wrote *The Tale of Peter Rabbit*. Mr. McGregor's garden is exactly as she described it. The door in the wall that the fat little rabbit could not squeeze underneath and the goldfish pool where the white cat sat twitching its tail are still there.

I had Camfield Place blessed when I came here in 1950 and was so happy with my husband until he died, and now with my children and grandchildren, that I know the atmosphere is filled with love and we have all been very lucky.

It is easy here to write of love and I know you will enjoy the Camfield Novels of Love. Their plots are definitely exciting and the covers very romantic. They come to you, like all my books, with love.

Bless you,

CAMFIELD NOVELS OF LOVE

by Barbara Cartland

THE POOR GOVERNESS
WINGED VICTORY
LUCKY IN LOVE
LOVE AND THE MARQUIS
A MIRACLE IN MUSIC
LIGHT OF THE GODS
BRIDE TO A BRIGAND
LOVE COMES WEST
A WITCH'S SPELL
SECRETS
THE STORMS OF LOVE
MOONLIGHT ON THE
    SPHINX
WHITE LILAC
REVENGE OF THE HEART
THE ISLAND OF LOVE
THERESA AND A TIGER
LOVE IS HEAVEN
MIRACLE FOR A MADONNA
A VERY UNUSUAL WIFE
THE PERIL AND THE
    PRINCE

ALONE AND AFRAID
TEMPTATION OF A
    TEACHER
ROYAL PUNISHMENT
THE DEVILISH DECEPTION
PARADISE FOUND
LOVE IS A GAMBLE
A VICTORY FOR LOVE
LOOK WITH LOVE
NEVER FORGET LOVE
HELGA IN HIDING
SAFE AT LAST
HAUNTED
CROWNED WITH LOVE
ESCAPE
THE DEVIL DEFEATED
THE SECRET OF THE
    MOSQUE
A DREAM IN SPAIN
THE LOVE TRAP
LISTEN TO LOVE
THE GOLDEN CAGE

LOVE CASTS OUT FEAR
A WORLD OF LOVE
DANCING ON A RAINBOW
LOVE JOINS THE CLANS
AN ANGEL RUNS AWAY
FORCED TO MARRY
BEWILDERED IN BERLIN
WANTED—A WEDDING
    RING
THE EARL ESCAPES
STARLIGHT OVER TUNIS
THE LOVE PUZZLE
LOVE AND KISSES
SAPPHIRES IN SIAM
A CARETAKER OF LOVE
SECRETS OF THE HEART
RIDING IN THE SKY
LOVERS IN LISBON
LOVE IS INVINCIBLE
THE GODDESS OF LOVE
AN ADVENTURE OF LOVE
THE HERB FOR HAPPINESS

Other books by Barbara Cartland

THE ADVENTURER
AGAIN THIS RAPTURE
BARBARA CARTLAND'S
    BOOK OF BEAUTY AND
    HEALTH
BLUE HEATHER
BROKEN BARRIERS
THE CAPTIVE HEART
THE COIN OF LOVE
THE COMPLACENT WIFE
COUNT THE STARS
DESIRE OF THE HEART
DESPERATE DEFIANCE
THE DREAM WITHIN
ELIZABETHAN LOVER
THE ENCHANTED WALTZ
THE ENCHANTING EVIL
ESCAPE FROM PASSION
FOR ALL ETERNITY
A GOLDEN GONDOLA
A HAZARD OF HEARTS
A HEART IS BROKEN
THE HIDDEN HEART
THE HORIZONS OF LOVE

IN THE ARMS OF LOVE
THE IRRESISTIBLE BUCK
THE KISS OF PARIS
THE KISS OF THE DEVIL
A KISS OF SILK
THE KNAVE OF HEARTS
THE LEAPING FLAME
A LIGHT TO THE HEART
LIGHTS OF LOVE
THE LITTLE PRETENDER
LOST ENCHANTMENT
LOVE AT FORTY
LOVE FORBIDDEN
LOVE IN HIDING
LOVE IS THE ENEMY
LOVE ME FOREVER
LOVE TO THE RESCUE
LOVE UNDER FIRE
THE MAGIC OF HONEY
METTERNICH THE
    PASSIONATE DIPLOMAT
MONEY, MAGIC AND
    MARRIAGE
NO HEART IS FREE
THE ODIOUS DUKE

OPEN WINGS
A RAINBOW TO HEAVEN
THE RELUCTANT BRIDE
THE SCANDALOUS LIFE
    OF KING CAROL
THE SECRET FEAR
THE SMUGGLED
    HEART
A SONG OF LOVE
STARS IN MY HEART
STOLEN HALO
SWEET ENCHANTRESS
SWEET PUNISHMENT
THEFT OF A HEART
THE THIEF OF LOVE
THIS TIME IT'S LOVE
TOUCH A STAR
TOWARDS THE STARS
THE UNKNOWN HEART
WE DANCED ALL NIGHT
THE WINGS OF ECSTASY
THE WINGS OF LOVE
WINGS ON MY HEART
WOMAN, THE ENIGMA

A NEW CAMFIELD NOVEL OF LOVE BY

BARBARA CARTLAND

The Herb for Happiness

JOVE BOOKS, NEW YORK

THE HERB FOR HAPPINESS

A Jove Book/published by arrangement with
the author

PRINTING HISTORY
Jove edition/September 1988

ISBN: 0-515-09705-5

Jove Books are published by The Berkley Publishing Group,
200 Madison Avenue, New York, New York 10016.
The name "JOVE" and the "J" logo
are trademarks belonging to Jove Publications, Inc.

PRINTED IN THE UNITED STATES OF AMERICA

10 9 8 7 6 5 4 3 2 1

Author's Note

HERBS have been known about all down the centuries, and especially by the Chinese. In England, Nicholas Culpeper, the very famous Astrologer-Physician of the early Seventeenth Century wrote a Complete Herbal which is still used today.

Throughout his life from 1616–1654 he devoted much of his time to the study of Astrology and medicine and published numerous tracts.

Although they were unorthodox and condemned by contemporary medical standards, they nevertheless enjoyed huge sales.

These herbal remedies are still of inestimable use today to everybody in the National Association for Health, of which I am the President. Since the Prince of Wales has recently announced his interest and approval of Alternative Medicine, it has become more popular than ever.

I started the National Association for Health in 1964 as a front for all the members and admirers of Alternative Medicine, and a great many people said that it was quite unnecessary.

Today it has a 250-million-pound turnover a year, with a third going in exports, and at the last Health Conference in 1983, thirty-eight countries were represented.

chapter one

1870

THE Duke of Mortlyn woke with a dry throat and a headache.

It infuriated him because he knew that last night, at Lady Bramwell's party, the champagne and the claret had not been wines he would have chosen for himself.

It annoyed him still more to know that Lord Bramwell, who was a rich man, was mean when it came to hospitality.

Nor did Lady Bramwell have the intelligence—although what woman had?—to choose good wines.

The dinner-party had been boring, but Doreen Bramwell had whispered that she had something important to talk to him about after the other guests had left.

The Duke was too experienced not to know what this meant, and he had debated with himself whether he should go or stay.

He was well aware that Lady Bramwell had been chasing him for some time.

Finally, since she was undoubtedly one of the most beautiful women in the whole of society, he had succumbed to the pleading in her eyes.

He had lingered after the other guests had said farewell.

It was then, with her arms around his neck and her

perfectly formed lips on his, that he had given in to the inevitable.

Now, as he realised that his Valet must have called him as usual at seven o'clock and left him sleeping, he knew that he had missed his usual ride in the Park.

It was not surprising that he had overslept.

He had not returned to his house in Park Lane until after dawn had broken and people were already moving about in the streets.

Now, as he stretched himself, he decided that he would not call on Lady Bramwell again as she expected him to do.

Despite that fact that the night had been fiery and everything a man could desire physically, there had been nothing new about it.

Because the Duke was so good-looking, extremely rich, and was in the Social circle, only one step down from the Royal Family, he had been cajoled, pursued, and chased by women ever since he had left Eton.

At thirty-three, he was still unmarried, and the pleadings of his family that he should take a wife had left him unmoved.

He had the unshakable conviction that if he married he would be bored.

Doubtless it would begin no more than two months after taking his bride down the aisle, which, in fact, would be longer than his *affaires de coeur* usually lasted.

"I am perfectly happy as I am."

He had said this only yesterday to his grandmother when she begged him once again to settle down and produce an heir.

"It is all very well to talk like that, Wade," she had replied, "but you know as well as I do that you cannot allow your tiresome cousin, Giles, to inherit the title."

"Certainly not," the Duke had agreed, "but I am not yet in my dotage, and when I am, I am sure with my

2

usual good luck I will supply you with several great-grandsons."

"I want them now," the Dowager Duchess had said firmly as the Duke laughed at her.

He got out of bed without ringing for his Valet and walked to the window.

The sun was shining on the trees in the Park and the sky was clear. It was going to be hot later in the day.

The Duke had a vision of the swans moving over the lake at Mortlyn.

He saw the gardens brilliant with flowers and the woods—which had protected the house for centuries—dark and mysterious as he had thought them to be when he was a boy.

"I will go to the country," he decided and rang the bell.

*   *   *

Half an hour later the Duke was downstairs finishing an excellent breakfast.

He was unaware that, as he was late, the Chef had cooked several dishes over again so that they would be exactly right the moment he appeared.

He was just finishing his second cup of coffee, when the door opened and his Secretary came in.

Mr. Watson had been with him since he had inherited the title and left the Army.

He was an extremely efficient man, so reliable and intelligent that he was the only person in whom the Duke really confided.

The son of the Headmaster of one of the more important Public Schools, Mr. Watson watched over the Duke and spared him any unnecessary problems.

In fact, he treated him in very much the same way as his father had treated the boys who had been in his charge.

"I apologise for bothering Your Grace," Mr. Watson

said, "but there is one thing which requires your attention."

"What is that?" the Duke asked uninterestedly.

Then, following his own train of thought, he said:

"Send the usual *bouquet* of flowers to Lady Bramwell and tell her that unfortunately I cannot call on her this evening as I am leaving for the country."

Mr. Watson made a note on a pad, then, lifting his eyebrows, he asked:

"Is Your Grace really going to Mortlyn?"

"I am bored with London," the Duke said almost petulantly. "The horses I bought at Tattersall's last week should have arrived by now. I want to try them out."

"Very well, Your Grace, I will make all the arrangements. You will, I imagine, wish to drive your Phaeton?"

"Of course," the Duke agreed, "with the new team of chestnuts."

He would have arisen from the table, then he remembered and asked:

"What was it you said needed my attention?"

"Actually it concerns Mortlyn."

The Duke frowned.

"No trouble, I hope?"

Mortlyn, his ancestral home, was very near to his heart. If he loved anything, he loved the huge Georgian house.

It had been erected by his grandfather on the site of an earlier Elizabethan building.

The estate which surrounded it consisted of twenty thousand acres, and the Duke liked to boast that he knew every inch of it and there was no other in the whole country to equal his.

"I told Your Grace last week," Mr. Watson said, "that the Vicar of Mortlyn Village had died."

"Yes, I remember," the Duke remarked. "You sent a wreath, of course?"

"Yes, Your Grace."

"I suppose now you are asking me to appoint another incumbent? Well, the Bishop knows exactly the sort of man I want."

"What I was actually going to ask Your Grace," Mr. Watson said, "was if it would be possible for you to provide the Vicar's daughter, Miss Linton, with a small house."

The Duke looked surprised before he said:

"I suppose it would be possible, but it is not something we do usually."

"Mr. Hunter, who Your Grace will remember looks after the almshouses, the pensioners, and all other buildings, has suggested the Dovecote."

The Duke looked astonished.

"The Dovecote?" he repeated. "Why should Hunter suggest that?"

"It would be suitable, Your Grace."

"Suitable for the daughter of a Vicar?" the Duke exclaimed. "It seems to me to be an extraordinary suggestion."

The Dovecote was in fact a house of which he was very fond.

It was small but pure Elizabethan and one of the oldest houses on the whole estate.

It had originally been the Dower House but had proved too small for the Dowager Duchesses.

A very much larger and more imposing building had been provided for them in the reign of George IV.

For some years, the Duke remembered, one of his great-aunts had lived in the Dovecote until she died.

Since then it had remained empty, but he was sure it was well looked after and well tended.

Now it seemed a revolutionary idea that someone from the village, even though she was the Vicar's daughter, should occupy what he had always thought of as a family residence.

Aloud he enquired:

"What possible qualifications can the Vicar's daughter have for aspiring to live at the Dovecote?"

He felt Mr. Watson was searching for words as he said:

"She has, Your Grace, preserved and extended the Herb Garden."

"I would have thought that was the job of the gardeners," the Duke snapped.

"They would not have been as knowledgeable as Miss Linton and known what to plant and what to retain."

"You think because she is interested in the Herb Garden, which I admit I have not seen for some years, she is entitled to be the tenant of the Dovecote?"

Mr. Watson moved a little uneasily.

It struck the Duke as extremely strange that he seemed somewhat hesitant, even nervous.

It was so unlike Watson, who was an extremely positive man and so quick-brained that the Duke always enjoyed talking to him.

"Come on, Watson," the Duke said, "tell me the truth. What is behind all this?"

Mr. Watson smiled and it made him look almost like a school-boy who had been trying to put something over on a Master.

"The truth is, Your Grace," he said, "Miss Linton is needed in the Village and, if she left, it would deeply distress everyone for miles."

"What does she do to make herself indispensable?" the Duke enquired. "Teach in the Sunday School, visit the sick? Good Heavens, Watson, there cannot be many invalids in such a small Village."

"There are very few, Your Grace, but that is due to Miss Linton."

"What are you saying? I do not understand!" the Duke almost snapped.

He had the feeling once again as he spoke that Watson—of all people—was being evasive.

To prompt his Secretary into telling him more, he said:

"I am certainly not going to let the Dovecote, which is without exception the most attractive small house I own on any of my estates, to any tiresome 'do-gooder' who wishes to hold Prayer Meetings in the Drawing Room."

As he spoke he had a picture of the Dovecote.

With its shallow bricks, mellowed with age, diamond-paned windows, and its rooms with their low ceilings supported by ships' wooden beams, it was very beautiful.

"I would hardly call Miss Linton that," Mr. Watson was replying, "although she does help people and, in fact, there is no-one more popular or more sought-after."

"Why?" the Duke asked.

"Because, Your Grace, she understands the use of herbs. Anyone who is injured or sick goes to her, as they went to her mother before she died, and is healed."

Mr. Watson took a deep breath and then, with what was obviously an act of bravery, said:

"They think of her, Your Grace, as a 'White Witch.'"

"Good God!" the Duke ejaculated.

Then he sat up straighter in his chair.

"Are you telling me, Watson, that in this day and age, when we are supposed to be more enlightened than we were in mediaeval times, that people still believe in witches?"

"I said a 'White Witch,' Your Grace, because where the Doctors fail, Miss Linton appears to effect almost magical cures."

The Duke sat back in his chair again.

"I suppose that in the country," he said, "where they have nothing to think about, the old superstitions are bound to linger on and people believe things that would be laughed to scorn elsewhere."

7

"I do not think that anyone would laugh at Miss Linton."

It was so unlike his Secretary to champion anyone who was not worthy of it, since usually he was far more sparing with his praise than his master, that the Duke was definitely intrigued.

Rising from the table, he said:

"I tell you what I will do, Watson. As I am leaving for Mortlyn in the next hour or so, I will see Miss Linton myself."

He paused before he added:

"I will then decide whether I consider her worthy of being allotted a cottage, when, as you well know, there is a great demand for them."

"I hope Your Grace will find something suitable," Mr. Watson replied.

The Duke was aware that his Secretary was thinking of the Dovecote.

But something obstinate within him made him determined, although he did not say so, that the Dovecote would remain empty.

He would certainly not allow some Parson's boring daughter to occupy it.

He was leaving the room, when Mr. Watson said hastily:

"There is something else, Your Grace."

"What is it now?" the Duke asked.

"Mr. Pearce, Your Grace's Accountant, asked me to bring to your notice that Mr. Digby has drawn cheques for no less than Four Thousand Pounds in the last two weeks."

"Four Thousand Pounds!" the Duke ejaculated. "What the devil can the boy be up to now?"

He did not wait for Mr. Watson to tell him, he knew.

His nephew, son of his elder sister, Oliver Digby, was infatuated by an alluring but extremely expensive Cyprian.

She was noted for being able to empty a man's

pockets more quickly than any of the other pretty young women in the same profession as herself.

'Four Thousand Pounds is too much,' the Duke decided.

As he walked into the Hall, he looked back over his shoulder and said sharply:

"Send a groom to tell Mr. Oliver I wish to see him, and to hurry, as I am leaving for the country."

"Very good, Your Grace."

The Duke walked into his Study, which was an attractive room on the ground floor looking out over the garden at the back.

It was decorated with a great number of books and a collection of sporting pictures which the Duke knew were the envy of his friends.

He sat down at his flat-topped desk, where there was a pile of letters waiting for him to sign.

There was a frown between his eyes.

There was no doubt that Oliver was a problem.

But he had promised his sister Violet, before she went off to India, where her husband had been made the Governor of a Province, that he would look after their son until they returned.

He was a very good-looking young man.

The Duke had expected that when he left Oxford, he would enjoy his position in the social world, and, of course, "sow his wild oats."

He had smiled understandingly when he was told stories of Oliver's riotous evening with his contemporaries.

He thought the noisy rows in night-clubs, Steeplechases at midnight, and a great deal of damage done after a drunken party were of no consequence.

All this was to be expected from a young man who had been let off the leash for the first time.

He had always thought that his sister-in-law had been over-protective and much too fussy about her only child.

At the same time, Four Thousand Pounds was a fortune.

His brother-in-law, Lord Digby, was a rich man, but he would find his position in India expensive and would not enjoy having to pay up on such a scale for his stepson.

'The best thing they could have done,' the Duke thought, 'was to take Oliver with them.'

He knew his sister had been reluctant to do that because she thought Oliver should move in the Social world to which he was entitled.

Now he would have the chance of meeting a nice girl whom he would marry.

Oliver, however, as the Duke had expected, found the pretty Cyprians more to his taste.

Ambitious mothers of *débutantes* had, of course, quickly added him to their lists of eligible bachelors.

Unfortunately they waited in vain for his appearance at the Balls and Receptions to which he was inevitably invited.

The Duke signed his letters and then looked somewhat disdainfully at a small pile, on the side, of letters addressed to himself which had not been opened.

He knew that with his usual perception Watson had realised that these were personal.

They were written to him by the women who affirmed far too positively that he had broken their hearts.

Pushing them over with one finger, the Duke recognised the flowery hand-writing of a Countess who had wept bitterly when he left her and continued to write to him reproachfully.

Another envelope, which carried the faint scent of gardenias, was from a Beauty who—he thought—had fallen into his arms far too quickly.

What the Duke enjoyed in his love affairs was the hunt and the chase rather than the inevitable end.

He had often asked himself why he was so cynical and far too frequently bored.

He knew it was because he was always searching for something he could not find.

He found it hard to express to himself what it was.

A lovely woman might attract him and he would feel, when he met her, a rising excitement.

It was much the same sensation as when he brought down right and left of grouse or stalked a magnificent Royal over the moors.

The trouble was that where women were concerned, he was invariably bored so soon.

It was because he knew, if he was truthful, that he was looking for something unusual, something that was not so banal that he not only knew every move of the game but also exactly what his "prey," if that was the right word for it, would say.

"What is the matter with me?" he often asked himself as he walked home from a house near his own when the dawn was breaking.

It was then he knew that instead of feeling happy, he was disappointed.

Last night there had been nothing unsatisfactory with the fiery exchange between himself and the beautiful Doreen.

Yet this morning, while he still admired her, he had no wish to touch her again.

He was quite certain that for the next two or three weeks, until she realised finally that she had failed to hold him, he would be bombarded with letters.

They would be cajoling, begging, pleading that he would see her.

Sometimes it seemed to him extraordinary that whilst almost every woman to whom he made love lost her heart, his—if he had one—was still intact and un-moved.

Because he had no wish to think about Lady Bram-well, or to open the letters on his desk, the Duke was relieved when the Butler announced:

"Mr. Oliver Digby, Your Grace."

His nephew came hurrying into the room.

Because he was so young, there were no signs of dissipation on his face.

The Duke, however, was sure that he had spent the night with his Cyprian and undoubtedly, if rumours were true, had indulged heavily.

"Good morning, Uncle Wade," Oliver said. "I am sorry if I kept you waiting, but I was asleep when your groom came hammering on my door."

"I imagined you would be," the Duke replied. "I am just going to the country and wanted to see you before I leave."

There was a wary look in Oliver's eyes as he asked:
"What about?"

"I think you know the answer," the Duke said. "You must be well aware that you are spending too much."

Oliver threw himself down into one of the comfortable armchairs.

"Things are very expensive in London at the moment," he said truculently.

"Especially somebody called Connie?" the Duke suggested.

"So you know about Connie!"

"I imagine it is no secret. In fact, the majority of people in London would know if they were interested. But quite frankly, she is too expensive for you."

"She is lovely and very amusing," Oliver protested.

"Not to the tune of Four Thousand Pounds," the Duke replied.

Oliver got up out of the chair and walked to the window to stare with unseeing eyes at the garden.

"All right," he said grudgingly after a moment, "if you are going to be unpleasant about it, I suppose I shall have to give her up."

"It is not a question of *my* being unpleasant," the Duke replied. "I am thinking of your step-father—it is he who eventually has to foot the bill."

Oliver turned round:

"You are not going to tell him?"

"You will have to do that," the Duke replied, "as soon as the Bank will no longer permit you to be overdrawn."

"Dammit!" Oliver exclaimed. "Why the hell can I not have money of my own and not have to go crawling to Papa for every penny I spend?"

The Duke knew that his brother-in-law had given Oliver a very generous allowance before he went to India.

He therefore thought this outburst was unfair, although he did not say so.

"What I was about to suggest," he replied, "was that as I am leaving for Mortlyn almost immediately, you might like to come with me."

"To the country—what on earth for?" Oliver enquired.

"I bought some horses at Tattersall's last week and I intend to try them out," the Duke explained. "I also thought some fresh air might be good for both of us."

Oliver considered this for a moment and then said:

"I think I should see Connie before I leave. I have rather committed myself to giving her a necklace she fancied."

"Can you afford it?"

"You know I cannot," Oliver answered, "but I did promise."

He looked at his uncle.

He was torn between doing the right thing where his step-father was concerned and disappointing a woman with whom he was infatuated.

"Save yourself from making such a momentous decision," the Duke said. "I will use my prerogative as your Guardian and order you to accompany me. If you explain that to Connie, she will understand."

"How do you know she will?" Oliver asked, sulking.

There was silence, then, as he saw a mocking smile on his Uncle's face, he said:

"Oh, my God, I never thought of that! Curse it, is there any woman in London who has not fallen for you?"

It was not a compliment. He walked towards the door and jerked it open before he said with deliberate rudeness:

"I will be ready to accompany Your Grace in fifteen minutes."

He slammed the door behind him and the Duke gave a little laugh.

As it happened, because he was very fastidious, he had made it a rule long ago never to patronise Cyprians or any woman who expected to be paid in cash for her favours.

However, because he was so rich, all the beautiful women with whom he spent his time expected to receive presents.

These were usually chosen by Mr. Watson with exceedingly good taste.

The Duke had lost count long ago how many sables, muffs, diamond bracelets, earrings, bags, sun-shades, and fans he had paid for.

They had certainly amounted to a very large sum over the years.

Oliver would learn in time, he thought, that women invariably asked for more than a man could afford.

It was just as much a mistake to be over-generous as it was to be niggardly.

Anyway, it would be a good thing for Oliver to accompany him to Mortlyn.

He thought that his sister would be grateful if she knew of all the trouble he was taking on her behalf.

*   *   *

The journey to Mortlyn took a little over two hours, although the Duke was always trying to improve on his own record.

14

When they drove past the ancient oaks, and the house lay just ahead of them, he was conscious of something like a thrill.

It was something he always felt when he saw his home.

Mortlyn was a grey stone building with a pillared front and wings stretching out on each side.

It was certainly one of the finest pieces of Adam architecture in the whole country.

The sun was glinting on the windows and the statues and urns which decorated the roofline were silhouetted against the blue of the sky.

There were green lawns sloping down to the lake.

The Duke invariably thought that it was even lovelier than when he had last seen it.

He had not spoken very much to Oliver on the journey.

He was more concerned with driving his new team with an expertise which made him outstanding.

Although he was not aware of it, he had the envy and admiration of all the young men about town.

As he crossed the bridge over the lake and drove up to the front-door, the groom, who was sitting behind him, said:

"Yer've done it again, Your Grace! Five minutes off the last time us came 'ere!"

"Five minutes?" the Duke repeated. "That is good, but not good enough. I had hoped for ten or fifteen."

"Your Grace'll do it sooner or later," the groom said confidently as he jumped to the ground before the wheels had stopped turning.

He need not have hurried, for, having been alerted that the Duke was arriving, two grooms came running to the horses' heads.

The red carpet was already laid over the steps and a number of Footmen in the family livery were in attendance.

The Duke walked slowly into the Hall, saying to the old Butler who greeted him:

"'Morning, Graves, is everything all right?'"

"It's delightful to see Your Grace again so soon," the Butler replied. "The champagne's in the Study and luncheon'll be ready in fifteen minutes."

"Good," the Duke approved. "Mr. Oliver and I are both hungry. We came straight from London without a stop."

"You are right, Uncle Wade. I did not have any breakfast this morning, so I am very hungry!" Oliver announced.

"As it would doubtless have consisted of a brandy and soda after a heavy night, that is a good thing," the Duke remarked.

"It is all very well for you," Oliver replied. "Everyone knows that you drink very little. But it is difficult to say 'No' when everyone else is swilling it down."

The Duke laughed.

He had not forgotten that, when he first sampled the delights of London life, he, too, had "swilled it down," as Oliver put it.

Then he had become aware that it affected his athletic pursuits, which were much more important.

His horses had always been more of a delight to him than anything else.

He was also an acknowledged pugilist.

Although it was out of fashion, he was additionally a swordsman who had tried his skill with the champions of Europe.

He wondered how he could persuade his nephew to take more exercise.

He knew it was something he should not be pressured into doing.

It would be better for him to enjoy the challenge and then, in consequence, keep his body fit and agile.

But he said nothing as Oliver drank three glasses of champagne to his one before luncheon was announced.

*　　*　　*

Later they inspected the horses.

Long before the Duke had finished going from stall to stall in the stables which housed nearly fifty outstanding animals, Oliver was beginning to yawn.

The Duke knew he was tired.

When he suggested that the young man might go to rest, and perhaps they would ride in the cool of the evening, Oliver readily agreed.

Then the Duke ordered one of his new stallions to be saddled and set off alone across the Park.

The horse was fresh, skittish, and determined to get the better of his new master.

It was the age-old battle between man and beast which the Duke enjoyed more than anything else.

In an hour the horse was completely under his control.

Then he remembered, as he saw the Church tower in the distance, what Mr. Watson had asked of him.

He told himself he would call on Miss Linton immediately and form his own opinion as to whether she was a "White Witch" or not.

He had a strong suspicion that she was just a tiresome woman preying on the stupidity of the local people, who had too little to think about.

Of course she made herself out to be much more important than she was.

He tried to remember what he knew about her father, who had died.

He recalled, after some thought, that as the Honourable Raymond Linton, the Vicar had been the third son of an impoverished Peer who lived in Huntingdon.

The Duke seldom went to Church, so he could not recall any of his sermons, but he had the idea that the Vicar had been an intelligent man.

He reckoned, as he drew nearer to the Church, that

Miss Linton must be getting on in years and he supposed that she had been unable to find a husband.

She had therefore consoled herself with herbs and other country remedies, pretending they were magic so as to call attention to herself.

It was the sort of thing which he thought was quite unnecessary in Little Mortlyn.

The Village contained the almshouses endowed by his great-grandfather, and a school built in memory of his grandfather.

There were also excellent cottages provided for the old servants once they were pensioned off.

Because the Village had always existed in the shadow, so to speak, of the Big House, it had—the Duke thought—a certain old-world charm.

It made it different from all the other Villages on his estate.

He had not thought of it before, but now he decided that he would be very particular who he put in the late Vicar's place.

Recommendations would, of course, come from the Bishop, but the final choice depended entirely on him.

Actually he felt rather guilty, as in other parishes he had left the choice to Mr. Watson, knowing he was a good judge of character.

However, where Little Mortlyn was concerned, the Duke was determined that he would do his own "picking and choosing."

If the first applicant the Bishop provided was not to his liking, he would tell him to try again.

The Church had originally been Norman and stood on the edge of the Park.

It was surrounded by ancient tomb-stones marking graves many of which the Duke saw to his satisfaction were adorned with colourful flowers.

He always thought of the village as if it were part of the house and the gardens, and his father had thought the same.

He remembered, when he was a boy, a frightful row because the grass had been allowed to grow too high in the Church-yard.

His father had even seen weeds along the path when he went to Church!

The Vicarage adjoined the Church-yard and was a pleasant-looking house, built about a hundred years earlier and approached by a small drive.

Shrubs were in blossom and the Duke noticed with approval that the flower beds in the front of the house were well-tended.

There was no-one to take his horse, but there was a post provided at the side of the door, where he was able to tie the reins to an iron ring.

He then walked into the Porch to find the front door was wide open.

There was a bell-chain beside it, and after he had pulled it sharply and listened, he could not hear the sound he expected coming from the Kitchen quarters.

Remembering the Vicar was dead, he imagined his daughter would either have one old servant or perhaps a woman who would have gone home by now.

The Duke walked into the small Hall.

Everything was brightly polished and there was a background smell of beeswax and lavender.

There was also a strong scent from a bowl of hyacinths which stood on a table at the bottom of the oak stairs.

It was certainly a point in Miss Linton's favour that he could find no fault with the house so far.

The Duke walked on to open the door of what he knew would be the Drawing Room.

It was empty, but the furniture was well-arranged and there were vases of flowers on several of the tables.

He decided that the door under the stairs would lead to the kitchen and walked in the other direction.

He opened the first door he came to and saw it had

obviously been the Vicar's Study, for the walls were lined with books.

He went on farther.

There was a room at the end of the short passage and, as he put his hand to the door, he thought he could hear someone speaking.

Since there seemed no point in knocking, he just opened the door.

The room was certainly not what he had expected.

There was a table down the centre and some other furniture.

There was what looked to be cages and boxes scattered about, and standing at the table a little way from him was a young woman.

The sunshine from the window turned her fair hair to gold.

She was busy with something which appeared to the Duke, at first glance, to be a bird.

Then a very soft, quiet voice said:

"Do not move or speak."

The Duke stopped.

It was not the way he was used to being spoken to, but he stood in silence.

After a minute or so the woman turned and now he could see clearly that she held in her hand a young cygnet.

She had obviously been fixing something to its wing.

She carried it across the room and set it down very gently in what was a roughly made cage.

"Now you will be all right," he heard her say in the same soft voice she would have used to a child. "In a few days you will be able to go back to your mother."

She closed the front of the cage, which was made of wire.

Then, as she turned round to look at him, he saw the expression of astonishment in her large eyes, which seemed to fill her whole face.

She was very young, merely a girl, and certainly not the woman he had expected her to be.

She was also, to his astonishment, extremely pretty.

Actually, "lovely" was the right word—in a different way from anyone he had ever seen before.

There was something fragile, perhaps ethereal, about her.

Her eyes slanted slightly at the corners, which gave her an elfin look, and this was echoed by her lips, which did the same.

She was wearing a big holland apron, and now she untied it and took it off to reveal a very simple cotton dress.

It fitted very tightly to her body and made her look even smaller and younger than she had before.

Then she spoke:

"I am . . . sorry, I did . . . not realise . . . I thought . . . you were . . . someone from the . . . Village."

"You are Miss Linton?"

The Duke thought, as he spoke, that there must be some mistake.

This lovely girl could not possibly be the late Vicar's daughter, whom he had expected to be getting on in years and trying to deceive simple folk into believing that she had magical powers.

"Yes, I am Selma Linton," the girl replied, "and I know that you are His Grace—the Duke."

As if she had suddenly thought of it, she made him a little curtsy which was a very graceful movement.

"I do not think we have ever met," the Duke said, moving a little farther into the room.

"I have seen you out hunting and admired your horses. Sometimes Hobson asks my advice if they are ill."

The Duke stared at her incredulously.

Hobson was his Chief Groom, and he found it hard to believe that Hobson would take anyone's advice, least of all that of a young woman who could not possibly presume to know as much as he did.

The Duke thought he was being deceived, and it annoyed him.

"I have come," he said in a lofty tone, "because I have been informed that you are asking me to provide you with a cottage in the Village."

Selma Linton was still for a moment, and then she answered, "Perhaps Your Grace would come into the Drawing Room. This is where I tend to the birds and animals and I am afraid there is nowhere to sit down."

The Duke looked round.

He could see, in one of the cages which was made out of a wooden box with netting in the front, that there was a small puppy.

In another there were two kittens, and in a third, a robin which had a small splint on one of its legs.

"Do you look after these creatures yourself?" he enquired.

"They go back to their owners or they are set free as soon as they are well."

He realised she did not want to talk about her skill.

She walked ahead of him through the open door and towards the Drawing Room.

He was again aware, as he followed her, of the fragrance of flowers and the scent of lavender.

"Will Your Grace please sit down," Selma enquired, and indicated an armchair by the side of the fireplace.

She paused and then went on:

"I am afraid the only refreshment I can offer you is some claret which Papa was given at Christmas—and I do not think that it is a particularly good vintage—or a cup of tea."

"Thank you, I need nothing," the Duke replied. "I have come, Miss Linton, to talk to you."

Selma seated herself on a chair opposite and put her hands in her lap.

She sat very gracefully, the Duke thought.

He was still puzzled, in fact bewildered, by her appearance.

He chose what he wished to say rather carefully:

"I have been told, Miss Linton, although it does not seem possible, that you have a reputation for doctoring the people in the Village with herbs."

He paused and continued:

"I was not informed that you also mended broken bones or, shall I say, in the case of a cygnet, wings."

Selma laughed. It was a very young and pretty sound.

"I suppose it sounds very grand put like that."

She smiled and then went on:

"My mother taught me all I know and I have been very grateful during my eighteen years, Your Grace, to have access to the wonderful ancient herbs which are grown in the Herb Garden of the Dovecote."

This, the Duke thought, was moving rather quickly.

He had not intended to speak of the Dovecote until he had made it quite clear that he was considering whether or not to let her have a cottage.

Playing for time, he looked round the room and said:

"I suppose everything here, the furniture and pictures, belongs to you?"

"The Vicarage was unfurnished when Papa and Mama came here fifteen years ago."

Selma's voice softened as she replied:

"They loved things which were old and beautiful, and it was a long time before the house was completely furnished."

As she spoke, the Duke realised that the furniture in the Drawing Room was extremely attractive.

He guessed that none of it had been very expensive, but the Lintons had obviously good taste and an educated appreciation of what was antique.

There was a Queen Anne inlaid walnut chest of drawers, a small Georgian table, and a Regency chair.

Over the years they had acquired pieces which he would have been pleased to own himself.

Selma watched the movement of his eyes and she said:

"Mama was an expert on furniture—Papa on pictures and books. So you can imagine that I am very . . . very lucky in what . . . they have . . . left me."

There was a note in her voice which told the Duke better than words that she missed her father and mother desperately.

He appreciated the fact that she was not trying to evoke his sympathy or telling him how unhappy she was.

Nevertheless, it was easy to read what she was feeling in her eyes, which were very expressive.

"I have been told," he said abruptly, "that you consider yourself a 'White Witch.'"

Again Selma laughed.

"I consider myself nothing of the sort, Your Grace."

She explained slowly so that he should understand:

"People like to twist what is just good common sense into magic and, if it makes them happy, I do not think it does any harm."

She looked at him hesitantly before she added:

"You must understand that if people believe they are going to get well, and one thing in particular will help, then that is half the battle."

"In other words, you are forcing people to believe in something supernatural?"

"I am doing nothing of the kind," Selma protested. "What most people need is hope and faith. If I give them hope, and if they think it comes from some Power greater than mine, that is, in fact, true."

She paused as if she expected him to contradict her, then went on:

"Papa believed that God gave us the Life Force, and if people wish to think the potency of the herbs I give them comes from the Power of God, that, if you think it out, is actually the truth."

The way she spoke made it a challenge. Because he could not help arguing, the Duke replied:

"I think, Miss Linton, you are making a very good case for deceiving people who are too stupid to understand that a herb is a herb, whatever fancy name you apply to it."

"A herb was also, Your Grace, created by God, grown by God, and—if it has healing powers—that is also given it by God. It is difficult to know where His work ends and mine begins."

The Duke was astonished.

It seemed impossible that this young girl should be able to answer him so quickly and without hesitation.

Nor was she so over-awed by him as to be tongue-tied.

Aloud he said:

"I had certainly not thought of it that way before, but perhaps if that is what you believe, it is under the circumstances reasonable."

"I thank Your Grace," Selma said, "and because there is less disease, less illness, less misery, and much more happiness in this Village than in any of the others round about, I hope . . . I may . . . stay . . . here."

"If that is true," the Duke replied, "I think that some of the credit should go to your Landlord for providing such good cottages."

"We are . . . very grateful . . . Your Grace."

Her eyes were twinkling and he had the feeling that she was laughing at him.

She was certainly not the least shy and he knew that she was the most unusual young woman he had ever met in his whole life.

Then, as she sensed he was criticising her, she bent forward in her chair:

"Please . . . Your Grace," she said in a very different tone, "let me stay. I have . . . nowhere else to go and . . .

as long as I am here . . . I feel I am . . . close to . . . Papa and Mama."

There was an expression of sincerity in her eyes which told the Duke that she was speaking from the very depths of her heart.

He rose to his feet, saying:

"I will tell you what I would like to do, Miss Linton."

She did not ask the obvious question, and he went on:

"I will call on you tomorrow morning and in my Phaeton. We will then go together and look at what cottages are available in the Village and see if there is anything suitable."

He looked round the room.

"I imagine you have too much furniture for most of them."

"I . . . suppose I could . . . store it."

The Duke walked towards the door.

He knew what they were both thinking—that the furniture would fit without any difficulty into the Dovecote.

But that was something which he did not wish to discuss.

He stopped in the Hall.

"Eleven o'clock tomorrow morning, Miss Linton, if that will suit you."

"I will be ready, Your Grace."

Selma dropped him a curtsy.

The Duke walked outside, released the bridle of his horse, and sprang into the saddle.

As he rode past the front-door where Selma was standing, he raised his hat and she curtsied again.

He thought how lovely she looked, framed by the ancient porch.

Then, as he rode on, he told himself that the whole thing was ridiculous.

How could a girl of that age gain a reputation for

healing, which Watson had undoubtedly exaggerated.

What was more, he was sure it was incorrect that a lady, which she undoubtedly was, should live alone in a cottage or anywhere else in the Village.

He had an uncomfortable feeling that he was up against something he did not understand.

The idea made him angry.

Spurring his horse, he rode faster than he had intended back to what he felt was the security and common sense of his own house.

chapter two

AFTER breakfast the following morning, the Duke sent for Mr. Hunter, who, as Mr. Watson had reminded him, was in charge of all the buildings on the estate.

He was a countryman who had served his father, and as the Duke knew, had a deep affection for Mortlyn.

He was an excellent rider and the Duke trusted him to exercise some of his most valuable horses, where he would not trust anyone else except his Chief Groom.

Mr. Hunter came respectfully into the Library, where the Duke was reading the newspapers.

"Good morning, Hunter."

"Good morning, Your Grace."

"I have decided today," the Duke said, "to inspect what cottages are available in the Village for Miss Linton."

There was an apprehensive look in Mr. Hunter's eyes, which puzzled him, but he went on:

"There is no question of her having the Dovecote, and I am surprised that you suggested it."

There was an uncomfortable silence and Mr. Hunter said:

"There is, Your Grace, a shortage of appropriate houses available for Miss Linton."

"Appropriate, what do you mean, appropriate? We

are under no obligation to house a Vicar's family when he can no longer officiate."

"I'm aware of that, Your Grace."

As the man obviously had nothing more to say, the Duke rose to his feet.

"Very well, Hunter, give me a list of the available cottages. I have promised to take Miss Linton to see them, and afterwards I will let you know what I have decided."

"I thank Your Grace."

Mr. Hunter put his hand into his pocket and brought out a piece of paper.

He gave it to the Duke, bowed respectfully, and left the Library.

When he had gone, the Duke thought that maybe he had been sharper than he meant to be.

Hunter was an excellent man and did his work to his satisfaction. He had never heard a word of criticism about him—which was unusual.

Nevertheless, he thought it was an impertinence to suggest giving Selma Linton anything so important to the family as the Dovecote.

"I suppose," he thought scornfully, "that as she is such a pretty girl, she has all the men running round her."

He walked towards his desk.

As he did so, he was aware that on top of the pile of letters which had arrived this morning was one he recognised as being from Doreen Bramwell.

He knew only too well that it contained a soft-worded reproach that he had been obliged to leave London and suggestions of when they could meet again.

It was something he had no intention of doing.

He therefore wondered how he could convey, without being brutal, that their affair—short though it may have been—was over.

Once again he was wondering why however beautiful

a woman might be she failed to hold his interest, and Doreen Bramwell was no exception.

Because he was irritated by his own thoughts, he picked up the piece of paper which Mr. Hunter had left for him.

Without opening it he put it into his pocket.

He looked at the clock and realised that it was too early for his Phaeton to be brought round.

He decided, instead, that he would go to the stables and discuss with Hobson the progress of his new horses.

He might perhaps change the pair he had intended driving for another.

It was first a vague idea in his mind as he walked from the Library into the Hall.

Coming down the stairs—late as he might have expected—was Oliver.

"Good morning, Uncle Wade," he said. "Do not rebuke me for over-sleeping—I was, in fact, dead tired. It was the first good night I have had for weeks."

The Duke laughed.

"I am not rebuking you, and I think that we went to bed early—and very sober—was the real reason for your sleeping the clock round."

"Now you are preaching at me!"

However, Oliver was not complaining but smiling at his uncle good-humouredly before he exclaimed:

"Are you going out? I had hoped that we could go riding."

"We will do that after luncheon," the Duke said. "I have an appointment this morning."

He paused and then continued:

"However, I am going to the stables and will order one of my horses on which you can work off some of your energy!"

"I would like that," Oliver replied, "but do not be away too long."

He walked towards the Breakfast Room.

The Duke proceeded along another corridor, which

led to a door at the end of the house, which was the nearest way to the stables.

He thought, as he entered the cobbled yard, that he had been right in bringing Oliver into the country.

Perhaps when they had dinner tonight he could talk to him seriously about his future.

* * *

Hobson, the Chief Groom, had a great deal to say about the horses.

It was, therefore, after ten o'clock before the Duke stepped into his Phaeton.

It was drawn by a team of jet black horses with Arab blood in them for which he had paid a very large sum.

As he knew it would take him less than ten minutes to reach the Vicarage, he realised he would be too early.

He therefore drove out of the back of the Stable Yard, where there was a road by which he could encircle the Park.

He would then come back into the Village from another part of his estate.

The sun was shining but there was a slight wind to take the heat out of the air.

Driving with his usual expert skill, the Duke could enjoy the sight of his broad acres, in which the crops were beginning to sprout.

He appreciated the woods, which he knew would provide him with good sport in the Autumn, and the stream in which there were a number of trout.

He thought it might be amusing to take Oliver fishing one day.

He remembered the thrill of catching his first trout—although a very small one—when he was eight years old.

As he drove on, he thought that every part of the estate evoked some memory of his childhood.

In the house, everywhere he went made him remember his mother, who had given all her love to her husband and her children.

It was impossible to think of her being promiscuous or deceitful, as the women were with whom he associated in London.

He knew, if he were truthful, that whilst he accepted their favours he despised them because they were unfaithful to their husbands.

They had forgotten any ideals or morals they might have had when they were young.

Then, because he had no wish to think of London at the moment but to enjoy being in the country, he concentrated on driving.

He drove through the twisting lanes with their hedges covered with honeysuckle and convolvulus.

* * *

At exactly eleven o'clock he turned his horses into the Vicarage drive and drew up outside the front door.

He was not surprised to find that Selma was waiting for him.

It was what he had expected because he thought that no-one in her position would be anything but thrilled at driving beside him in his Phaeton.

At the same time, women were invariably unpunctual.

She hurried down the steps and, without waiting for him to alight—which may have been difficult without anyone to hold the horses—climbed up into the Phaeton.

She moved so quickly and gracefully that he felt she almost flew to him on wings.

He appreciated that she was looking exceedingly pretty in a simple pale blue cotton frock.

She wore a small straw bonnet which seemed almost like a halo for her fair hair and pointed face.

As he looked at her, he realised that he had forgotten

the strange way that her lips and her eyes slanted slightly upwards at the corners.

He wondered if, in fact, her obsession with herbs was because she had some resemblance to fairies and elves.

When he was little, his mother had told him they left circles of mushroom rings in the woods where they had danced.

Then he thought he was being too imaginative about this Vicar's daughter.

"The sooner I find her a cottage," he told himself, "and forget about her, the better."

He drove carefully out of the drive, as the gates were not very wide.

As they went towards the village he pulled out of his pocket the paper which Mr. Hunter had given him and handed it to Selma.

"You will find the cottages which are available written on this piece of paper," he said. "I want you to direct me to them, as I am not sure where they are situated."

Selma took the paper from him and, before she opened it, she said:

"First I must thank you, Your Grace. It is very exciting to ride with you in your Phaeton."

"It is something you wished to do?" the Duke asked.

"But of course," she replied. "When I see your magnificent horses, I ride them in my dreams."

She laughed as she spoke.

He was aware that she was not, as any other woman might have been, trying to cadge an invitation to his stables.

"Now that one of your dreams has come true," he said dryly, "where do we go first?"

Selma opened the piece of paper and then there was a little silence before she said in a rather strange voice:

"There is the name of only one cottage here."

"One?" the Duke asked. "I told Hunter to give me the names of all those available."

"That is exactly what Mr. Hunter has done, Your Grace."

There was a pause before the Duke asked:

"Well, where is it?"

"At the other end of the Village. It is called Bleak Cottage and has not been lived in for many years."

"Why not?"

Again there was a pause before Selma said:

"A murder was committed there over a hundred years ago, and people have been afraid of it ever since."

The Duke looked at her in astonishment:

"Are you telling me the cottage is derelict?"

"You must see for yourself, Your Grace."

"Then why did Hunter not tell me?"

Even as he spoke he knew the reason. Hunter was eager that Miss Linton should live in the Dovecote.

This made him more determined than ever that he would leave the Dovecote empty.

They drove on through the pretty Village with its thatched cottages and small gardens bright with flowers.

'It really is,' the Duke thought with satisfaction, 'a model of its kind.'

The people they passed at first stared at Selma seated beside him and then waved in a friendly fashion.

It was, he knew, something they would not have done if he had been alone.

The pretty cottages came to an end and, after they had passed the almshouses, they proceeded a quarter of a mile farther up the road, where there were no buildings.

Then, standing back in an overgrown plot which once must have been a garden, was Bleak Cottage.

There was no need to inspect it.

The roof had fallen in, there was no glass in any of the windows, and the building was, in fact, nothing but a shell.

'Even to go near it,' the Duke thought, 'might be dangerous!'

"I suppose," he said aloud, as Selma did not speak, "that this is Hunter's idea of a joke."

"Please do not be angry with him," Selma pleaded.

She paused and then went on:

"You asked him to provide you with the names of empty cottages available in the Village. This is, in fact, the only one."

Then she gave him one of her strange little smiles before she said:

"Everyone wants to live in Little Mortlyn."

"Why?" the Duke asked.

"Without flattering Your Grace," Selma replied, "you are known to be a very good landlord."

She hesitated, then continued:

"Also, I think you will understand when I tell you that when Papa and Mama were alive, they made everyone in the Village feel that they were part of one big family."

"Your father and mother are now dead," the Duke said, "and, if you want to stay, we will have to find you somewhere to live."

The answer was obvious and he waited to see what Selma would suggest.

She made a helpless little gesture with her hands before she said:

"I suppose . . . Your Grace . . . I shall . . . have to . . . go away."

"There must be someone who will have you—somewhere you can go."

Selma did not speak, and after a moment the Duke said:

"Who are your mother's relatives? Surely there is one person among them who would offer you a home?"

He knew he was being harsh in the way he was speaking.

Yet, he told himself that he would not be pressured

into giving Miss Linton the Dovecote, whatever Hunter, Watson, or anyone else might say.

'The whole thing is ridiculous,' he thought. 'This girl is not my responsibility.'

She was obviously thinking how to reply to his question, and after a long hesitation she said:

"It is very . . . difficult. My grandfather lives in the North of Scotland . . . he is very old. When Mama married . . . my father, Grandfather was . . . extremely angry."

"Why should he have been?"

"Because Papa was a Sassenach. I know that Your Grace has been to Scotland and you must be aware that many Scots hate the English."

The Duke knew this was true, and he asked:

"What is your grandfather's name?"

"Lord Nabor and he is Chieftain of the McNabor clan."

The Duke was astonished.

He was well aware of the importance of the Scottish Chieftains, even though many of them were impoverished, with their Castles crumbling about their ears.

"And you think that your grandfather would not welcome you because you have English blood in your veins?"

Selma clasped her hands together.

"Oh, please . . . Your Grace . . . I have no wish to live in Scotland but only to stay . . . here with the people whom I have known since I was . . . a baby."

The Duke did not reply, and she said as though she were speaking to herself:

"They love me . . . I know they do . . . and if I left, they would . . . miss me."

"What you are saying," the Duke said scathingly, "is that they would miss the herbs which you have told them are magical, and what they think of as their 'White Witch.'"

Selma did not reply, and he felt suddenly as if he had

36

struck something small and vulnerable and that it had been a very unsporting thing to do.

He tightened his reins:

"As I have heard so much about these herbs and the garden from which they come," he said, "we will go and look at it."

He could not restrain the irritated tone in his voice.

He had the feeling, as he drove on, that Selma was fighting against the tears which had come into her eyes.

"That is typical of a woman," he told himself savagely. "When they cannot get their way they cry. They expect, because they look pathetic, that a man will give into them."

That was one thing he was not going to do.

If the worse came to the worst, he would build a cottage for Selma.

Under no circumstances would she have the Dovecote.

They drove in silence through the wrought iron gates with their two Georgian Lodges on either side of them.

They went a little way up the drive itself, then the Duke turned to the left and, nearly half a mile across the Park, they came to the Dovecote.

The garden was encircled with ancient trees, and on his orders the lawns were kept smooth and green.

The yew hedges were clipped and the topiary figures of birds were in perfect condition.

The house itself, he thought, looked even lovelier than he remembered.

There was the weathered pink of the shallow Elizabethan bricks, the gabled diamond-paned windows, and the door, with the date carved in stone above it, was a picture in itself.

There was a gardener, who belonged to Mortlyn, working in front of the house.

He straightened himself as he saw the Phaeton approach.

When he realised it was driven by his Master, he hurried to the horses' heads.

The Duke alighted from the Phaeton and went round it to help Selma to the ground, but she had already jumped down before he could reach her.

She patted one of the horses.

"Good morning, Ben," the Duke heard her say to the gardener, "is your mother better?"

"Her be better than Oi've ever known her be, thanks to ye, Miss," Ben replied.

She realised that the Duke had joined them and looked up at him to say:

"Your horses are magnificent, just as I had expected them to be."

"Because they are mine?" the Duke enquired.

All the women he knew in London would have answered in the affirmative.

They would also have added that the horses were as magnificent as he was himself.

Selma only replied in an impersonal tone:

"It is what everyone expects from the stables of Mortlyn."

She patted the other horse and then asked:

"Shall I take you to the Herb Garden?"

"That is why we are here," the Duke replied.

She went through an archway in the red brick wall at the side of the house.

First there was a rose garden, with an ancient sundial in the centre of it.

Then through another brick wall on the other side was a small garden, in the centre of which there was a fountain.

It was not playing, but the water would have come from a Cornucopia held in the arms of Eros.

The stone basin was carved with small fat Cupids carrying, instead of garlands of flowers and fruit, what the Duke thought were herbs.

It was very ancient and he was sure it had been

erected at the same time as the house had been built and the Herb Garden begun.

He had expected it to be well-kept and he saw that, in fact, the small beds between box hedges were in perfect order.

What was more, every available inch of soil had been planted.

Despite himself, he was impressed.

"Are you responsible for this?" he enquired.

Selma shook her head.

"No, it was Mama who planted everything so carefully and who told me exactly which crop of herbs was to follow another."

The Duke did not answer and, after a moment, Selma said in a low voice:

"Always when I come . . . here I feel Mama is . . . beside me, guiding me and . . . telling me . . . what I must . . . do."

The Duke was conscious of the buzzing of the bees, and the song of the birds in the trees just outside the garden.

There was a scent in the air which was different from anything he had known elsewhere.

While the garden was beautiful, at the same time he was aware that, to Selma, it had a special significance.

It was almost as if a voice inside him told him that she believed that everything which grew there was for the good of other people.

As he thought somewhat uneasily that he was being mesmerised by what he saw, he said:

"I must commend you, Miss Linton, on the work you have done here. I can understand that you do find it invaluable in what you must think of as your chosen profession."

He was speaking in a lofty, almost cynical manner, which he was aware some people found intimidating.

Then, to his surprise, Selma turned away.

She began to walk back through the opening in the wall through which they had come.

To his annoyance, he was aware that she thought he was profaning what to her was sacred.

She wanted, although it seemed incredible, him to come away from the garden as quickly as possible.

He had no idea how he knew this, at the same time, he told himself that it was an impertinence on her part.

As the garden was his, how dare she be so possessive of it?

Then, before Selma reached the entrance, a man appeared and came hurrying towards them.

Aware of his haste, the Duke looked at him in surprise and realised that it was Hunter.

He did not move from the fountain where he had been standing, and Mr. Hunter ran down the paved path to the Duke's side.

"Your Grace," he said breathlessly, "you are wanted . . . back at the house . . . immediately."

"What has happened and why are you in such a hurry?"

"It is Mr. Oliver, Your Grace. He was coming out of the front door to go riding, when a statue fell from the roof."

The Duke stared in astonishment before he said:

"A statue fell from the roof—I do not believe it!"

"It would have killed Mr. Oliver if it had fallen on his head, but just as he was coming out of the door he turned back to get his whip and that saved his life."

"But he is injured?" the Duke questioned.

"The statue caught him on the back of one leg, Your Grace, as he was taking a long stride forward with the other, and it is badly damaged."

"You have sent for the Doctor?"

"The Doctor is away, Your Grace," Mr. Hunter replied, "and will not be back for several days."

He paused for breath and then continued:

"I have come for Miss Selma. They told me at the

Vicarage that she was out driving with you and I guessed she would be here."

He looked at Selma as he spoke, who had been listening.

"You will be able to help him," he said.

It was a statement.

"There must be some Doctor . . ." the Duke began to say.

To his astonishment, he realised that neither Selma nor Hunter were listening to him.

She was asking in a low voice for more details of the injury, and Hunter was telling her in the same breathless voice which he had used since he arrived.

"He must be in great pain and I expect he has lost a lot of blood," Selma said.

"They were carrying him upstairs when I left the house," Mr. Hunter said. "Mr. Graves said to me: 'Get Miss Selma and be quick about it.' So I wasted no time asking questions."

"That was sensible."

She ran from Mr. Hunter's side and started picking herbs—first from one bed then from another.

The Duke moved closer to Mr. Hunter and said to him:

"This is ridiculous, there must be a Doctor somewhere in the vicinity."

"Miss Selma'll know what to do, Your Grace."

The Duke was about to argue, when Selma came running back to them with a bunch of herbs in her hand.

She looked at the Duke and he knew, without words, that she expected him to drive her to the house.

She went ahead of the two men and crossed the rose garden towards the Phaeton.

She was already sitting in it by the time the Duke and Mr. Hunter arrived. The Duke stepped into it and took up the reins.

Mr. Hunter hurried towards his horse, which was standing unattended on the grass lawn.

He mounted but waited until the Duke drove off.

Then once they were out of the drive he rode as swiftly as he could through the Park towards the house.

* * *

As Mr. Hunter rode directly over the Park, he arrived at the house before them and was waiting at the top of the steps when the Duke pulled his horses to a standstill.

Selma alighted almost before the wheels stopped moving.

Then as she ran round the Phaeton, the Duke also reached the ground.

They started to climb the steps side by side.

"I have ascertained, Your Grace," Mr. Hunter said as they reached him, "that Mr. Oliver has been taken to his own room and Mrs. Fielding and Your Grace's Valet are with him."

The Duke did not reply.

He was doing his best to keep up with Selma, who seemed almost to float up the steps and across the Hall.

She moved up the Grand Staircase as if her feet did not touch the stairs.

The bedrooms which the Duke and his principal guests used were on the first floor.

It was quite a distance from the front-door, but they reached Oliver's bedroom more quickly than the Duke would have believed.

It was known as The Prince's Room, and he thought it strange that Selma did not ask where it was.

Then he told himself that every detail of everything that happened in the Big House was discussed in the Village.

He was sure that everyone was aware that The Prince's Room was used by Oliver every time he came to Mortlyn, just as Queen Adelaide's Room was known to be his mother's.

When they entered The Prince's Room, the Duke

was not surprised to find it filled with servants.

There was Groves, the Butler, Mrs. Fielding, the Housekeeper, several housemaids, two Footmen, and Daws, his Personal Valet, who was always invaluable in a crisis.

When the Duke and Selma entered the room, they moved back from the bedside.

The Duke was aware that they were not looking at him but at Selma.

Oliver had been, as Mr. Hunter said, carried upstairs after the accident.

His riding-boot had been cut off and he had been undressed except for his shirt.

A blanket covered his body.

His leg, which had been badly crushed and was bleeding profusely, was exposed at the foot of the bed.

He was groaning in agony and turning his head from side to side as if the pain were intolerable.

Without taking any notice of the people in the room, Selma went to the bedside.

Bending over Oliver, she said in the soft voice which the Duke had heard her use to the cygnet:

"It is quite all right, the pain will soon pass and you must be very brave."

"I cannot—bear it—I cannot," Oliver muttered.

"I know," Selma said. "But try to think of something else, something you like or love."

She put her hand on his forehead.

As if she realised that he was cold, she pulled the blanket—which was folded only to his waist—up higher.

She then moved to look at his leg, which the Duke thought was so horrifying that most women would have fainted at the sight of it.

The statue which had fallen from the roof had crashed onto the back of one boot and inflicted terrible damage.

If it had hit him on the head, it would certainly have killed him.

The skin of his leg was churned up and still bleeding, although no artery seemed to be involved.

His ankle was twisted sideways, which told the Duke that it was broken.

Selma looked at it for a long moment before she said:

"Mrs. Fielding, will you make a syrup from these herbs as you did for my mother when His Late Grace broke his collar-bone."

"Yes, Miss Selma, I remembers. I'll see to it."

Selma placed in the Housekeeper's hands some of the herbs which she carried and then added:

"As quickly as you can. It will relieve Mr. Oliver's pain and then I can set his ankle."

The Duke was about to interrupt, but Selma looked at one of the footmen and said:

"James, I want a splint exactly the same length and size as the one I used on your brother."

"Oi remembers, Miss."

"Please hurry, and make it smooth."

"And Emily," Selma said to the elder housemaid, "will you and Amy start tearing up a fine linen sheet for bandages? I want them two or three inches wide."

"Yes, Miss."

The housemaids followed Mrs. Fielding from the room. James had already gone.

Selma looked again at the damaged leg before she said to Graves:

"We shall have to be certain that there are no fragments of leather left after we have cleaned this."

She paused and then continued:

"I know you will find some Hawthorn flowers in bloom in the garden and, if we use them before we apply the honey, it will draw them out."

Graves gave the Duke an embarrassed look before he replied:

"Yes, Miss, I'll go and do that at once."

That left only the Duke, Daws, and Selma.

"Now the only other thing I need," Selma said, "is honey. If you go to the Still-Room, you will find Mrs. Burrows there."

She paused and then continued:

"A thick honey is best, and she will have some clover honey left over from last year."

Daws hesitated for a moment as though he thought he should ask his Master's permission.

He then decided it was not a time to stand on ceremony and hurried away as the rest of the servants had done.

Selma moved again to Oliver's side.

All the time she had been giving her instructions, he had been groaning, although not as loudly as he had before she had arrived.

As she put her hand on his forehead and moved it gently, it seemed to quieten him.

The Duke would have spoken, but he realised that Selma was concentrating so completely on what she was doing that it was doubtful if she would even have heard him.

He watched her and, after a few moments, he was aware that she was praying.

Without taking her hand from Oliver's forehead, she pulled off her bonnet and threw it carelessly on the floor.

Then, with her eyes shut, she went on gently massaging and praying until Oliver's groans became only a whimper.

One by one the servants came back, but Selma took no notice until Mrs. Fielding appeared.

She carried a glass in her hand. As she handed it to Selma she said:

"I've made it exactly as I did before, Miss, and was very careful with the poppy."

The Duke started. He was well aware that from poppy heads opium could be extracted.

He had not travelled in the Orient without knowing how dangerous this could be.

He was wondering whether he should warn Selma not to use it.

As if she were aware of what he was thinking, she said before he could speak:

"Wild Poppy is quite safe if only very little is used and it is mixed with Rue, Coralwort, and *Fleur-de-Lys*."

She took the glass from the Housekeeper and felt it to see if it was the right temperature.

She raised Oliver's head in what the Duke realised was a very experienced way.

"I want you to drink this," she said in her quiet, almost hypnotic manner. "It will make you sleep and the pain will go away."

She continued softly:

"It is not very nice, but I know that you will be very brave and drink it down because it will do you good."

Almost like a child Oliver drank the contents of the tumbler, and only when he had done so did he mutter:

"That—was—filthy!"

"I know it was," Selma replied, "but now go to sleep."

She went on very quietly:

"Think that you are lying in the sun and the warmth of it is taking away your pain, healing your leg. Also you are riding one of your uncle's magnificent horses. Think of it, think of the horse beneath you and how much you enjoy the ride."

The movement of her hand on his forehead seemed to grow slower and finally, when she stopped, the Duke realised that Oliver was asleep.

He was undoubtedly drugged by the herbs Selma had given him and perhaps hypnotised by the movement of her hand.

The Duke was so intent on watching Selma that he had not realised that all the other servants, sent on their various errands, had now come back into the room.

For the first time since they had entered the bedroom Selma looked at him.

"Will you stand beside your nephew, Your Grace? If he moves, you must hold him down. Otherwise, please do not touch him."

Obediently, because there was nothing else he could do, the Duke went to the top of the bed.

He heard Selma talking to Daws in a low voice.

Then, to his astonishment, he saw her grasp Oliver's mangled, blood-stained leg firmly.

With a quick twist of her hands as Daws held his knee she set his ankle.

She did it so neatly, so cleverly, that he could hardly believe that the ankle was back in place.

She and Daws then washed the leg very carefully, removing pieces of stocking which had been crushed into his leg.

Then they sprinkled it very gently with the Hawthorn water.

To the Duke's surprise, Selma then covered the entire wound with a thick application of clover honey.

She used two pots before the leg was completely coated with the honey.

The housemaids produced their bandages and pieces of linen, which Selma made into pads.

She attached the splint very carefully, padding it so that it could not possibly hurt what was left of the skin.

Afterwards the entire limb was bandaged from the knee downwards.

It took some time, but to the Duke's relief, Oliver never moved until their work was completed.

When the blood-stained sheets were taken away and fresh ones put very carefully in their place, Selma looked down with satisfaction at the leg.

Tidily encased as it was in an extra piece of linen, it was hard to remember the mashed, blood-stained horror it had been before.

Selma pulled a blanket very lightly over it.

As she finished she smiled at Daws:

"Thank you, you were very helpful."

"I've never seen anythin' like this afore, Miss," Daws replied, "'though I've treated a lot o'wounds in m' time."

"I thought you would have, as I knew you had been with His Grace in the Army."

"Daws is, in fact, an excellent Nurse," the Duke joined in.

"You have all been very kind."

Selma paused and then went on:

"I do not want the bandages changed for forty-eight hours, unless, of course, Mr. Oliver complains."

Her voice was serious as she said:

"We have to do everything possible to prevent him from being restless until his bone has set."

"Do you want him to keep on with th' herbs, Miss?" Mrs. Fielding asked.

"I have some more here which I should like you to use. But you must throw away what is left of the syrup made from the poppies. He must not have any more."

"I understands," Mrs. Fielding replied.

The Duke felt almost as though he had stepped into another world—one of which he knew nothing.

"Surely," he said to Selma, "you want a Doctor to see him?"

"If that is Your Grace's wish, but I think it would be a great mistake to remove the bandages, or to put anything else on his leg except honey until it has begun to heal."

"I cannot believe that is the right treatment," the Duke replied.

"Oh, but it is, Your Grace!" Emily said as if the words burst out of her. "Everyone in the Village'll tell you that honey 'eals wounds, cuts, an' burns."

She paused and then went on:

"When my little niece was almost scalded to death

48

after a kettle tipped over 'er, t'were honey that saved her from dying from th' pain. Her skin grew again just like a newborn babe's."

Emily had spoken impetuously, then, as if she felt she had been too forward, she dropped a curtsy as she added:

"If Your Grace'll excuse me for saying so."

The Duke looked at Selma with an almost mocking smile on his lips as he said:

"I see I must bow to your superior knowledge."

She did not reply, and he went on:

"Now I want to know more about how this accident happened. So I suggest, Daws, that you look after Mr. Oliver while I go downstairs to learn exactly what occurred."

He saw Selma look at him and, as if she had asked a question, he added:

"You come with me. I think you should really have known what had happened before you treated the result of the accident."

She thought she smiled as if that was unnecessary and he was deliberately finding fault.

The Duke walked out of the room, followed by Selma and Graves.

They went slowly down the staircase up which they had come so hurriedly, and walked out of the front door.

The Duke found, as he had expected, that the statue which had fallen on Oliver had been removed from the place where it struck him to the side of the wide steps.

It had been propped against the stone balustrade which curved downwards with heraldic figures at the top and bottom of it.

Mr. Hunter was there and also Mr. Watson, who had arrived from London early that morning.

He always moved to whichever house the Duke was in residence, as His Grace trusted no-one but him with his correspondence and engagements.

The two men stood at one side to allow the Duke to

look at the statue, which was of Diana, Goddess of the Chase.

It was one of the statues which had been erected at the time the house was built.

The Duke always had them inspected every year, and he knew that they had been seen by an expert when the last winter was over.

His report had stated there was no deterioration and certainly no likelihood of any of them falling to the ground.

"What do you think of it, Watson?" he asked his Secretary, having already made up his own mind.

"Mr. Hunter and I were just saying, Your Grace, it is quite obvious that the statue has been deliberately cut loose from its pedestal."

"That is what I thought myself," the Duke said. "In God's name, who would do such a thing?"

There was a moment's silence and the Duke knew that was what the two men had been talking about before his arrival.

"Well?" he asked sharply.

"I think, Your Grace, it is something we should discuss in private."

The Duke looked at him in astonishment.

"Are you really telling me," he said, "that there was someone up on the roof who deliberately pushed the statue over when Mr. Oliver appeared?"

"I think, Your Grace," Mr. Hunter intervened, "that as it was your horse waiting below, it was you whom the culprit expected to go riding."

The Duke stared at Hunter before he said:

"Are you implying that someone was intending to kill me?"

"Yes, Your Grace."

"I cannot believe it!"

Once again Mr. Hunter looked at Mr. Watson:

"We have no proof, Your Grace."

"No-one saw anyone on the roof?" the Duke asked as

if he had no wish to agree with their contention.

"The stable-lad who came with the horse," Mr. Hunter said, "told us that he saw someone move on the roof before the statue began to topple."

"It seems almost incredible," the Duke said.

He was aware as he spoke that Selma had been standing just behind him listening to the conversation.

Then she said in her quiet little voice:

"I think Your Grace has had a very lucky escape. Your nephew's leg will heal quickly. Fortunately, I understand, he turned back to get his whip."

She paused before she said in a very serious voice:

"If the statue had fallen on his head, or yours, there would have been no chance of survival."

"Are you suggesting, Miss Linton," the Duke asked mockingly, "that I should be grateful to be alive?"

"But, of course, Your Grace, could you be anything else?"

She looked at him reproachfully as she spoke.

Once again he thought that she was the most unusual and extra-ordinary woman he had ever met in his whole life.

Then, as if she had seen everything she wanted to, she walked back into the house and he knew that she was returning to her patient.

chapter three

THE Duke was in his Study when Mr. Watson came into the room.

He had been signing his letters and looked up as his Secretary approached to ask:

"Well, Watson, what have you discovered?"

"I am afraid, Your Grace," Mr. Watson replied, "that it is what we suspected."

"I want every detail."

"One of the gardeners is quite certain, Your Grace," replied Mr. Watson, "that he saw Mr. Giles the previous night driving through the Village."

"Was he absolutely sure?"

"Emery is a very truthful man, Your Grace, who has been with us for fifteen years."

The Duke nodded and Mr. Watson continued:

"I have questioned the stable-lad, who said Mr. Oliver turned round to get his whip and by doing so saved his own life."

He paused as if to make what followed more impressive.

"He is absolutely convinced, Your Grace, that there was a man on the roof and he saw his shoulder quite clearly just before the statue toppled over."

The Duke's mouth tightened into a hard line and he

did not say anything as Mr. Watson continued:

"I can only beg of Your Grace to be very careful. I have not told you before, but Mr. Giles is in deep water."

"Money?" the Duke enquired.

"Yes, Your Grace, and there has been a rumour—although I cannot substantiate it—that he is borrowing from Usurers on the assumption that you will not live long."

The Duke sat bolt upright in his chair.

"Is that the truth?"

"As I said, Your Grace, it is only a rumour," Mr. Watson replied, "which was reported to me by one of Your Grace's friends who was very concerned about you."

"You did not tell me."

"I did not do so, Your Grace, because Captain Seymour wanted to make further enquiries before we alerted Your Grace to the danger."

The Duke was silent.

He was realising only too clearly that if, as Giles had anticipated, he had come out through the front-door to go riding and the statue had fallen on him, he would now be dead and his cousin Giles would now be the Fifth Duke of Mortlyn.

He knew that, like himself, Watson was thinking that it was almost impossible to ensure complete protection in such a large house and over such a vast acreage.

The situation would be no better in London.

The Duke rose to his feet and walked to the window.

His Secretary regarded his broad shoulders and his well-poised head with a compassionate look in his eyes.

He was thinking that it was impossible for any man to have a more difficult problem to face and to solve than the one which confronted the Duke at this present moment.

There was no need for either of them to put into

words what an utter disaster it would be if Giles Lyne inherited the Dukedom.

He was now thirty-eight and, from the moment he grew up, he had spent his time with raffish men and immoral women and his money on them.

He had caused scandal after scandal in social circles.

No-one would have taken the slightest notice of him if he had not boasted loudly and consistently that he was Heir Presumptive to the Duke of Mortlyn.

The Duke himself had said openly, and now it appeared unwisely, that he had no wish to be married.

It had become a joke in White's Club, to which the Duke belonged and from which Giles had been black-balled, that he was the Elusive Bridegroom.

Any woman who caught him would have to be beautiful, sharp-witted, and far out of the ordinary.

There had been, of course, speculation after speculation as to whether the Duke would fall for the latest Beauty to appear on the London scene, or whether some attractive widow with whom he was seen more than once would succeed where others had failed.

Mr. Watson was aware, because he kept a sharp eye on Giles Lyne, that the years of extravagance and dissipation were beginning to take their toll.

He looked far older than his years and he was falling deeper and deeper into debt.

A number of his creditors had sought Mr. Watson to ask the Duke to save them from bankruptcy.

In the majority of cases Mr. Watson had thought it was the fault of the Coach-Builders, the Wine-Sellers, Tailors, and dozens of other tradesmen to have trusted anyone so obviously unstable as Mr. Giles.

But there had been one or two small shop-keepers who had been deceived by his boastful lies and on whose behalf Mr. Watson had elicited the Duke's help.

The Duke had paid up, but had made it clear to his cousin that he would not be responsible for his future debts and this sort of situation was not to occur again.

Giles had not been in the least grateful.

He had merely taken the money and defamed the Duke behind his back.

He called him a "skinflint," a "Ducal cheeseparer," and did his best to make him a laughing-stock.

Fortunately the only people who listened to him were his few particular cronies, most of them no more than toadies.

The rest of London Society was shocked at his behaviour and ostracized him completely.

It was, in fact, the Duke's grandmother who was most distressed by what had occurred.

Her solution was that the Duke should marry as quickly as possible and have an Heir.

Now the Duke himself was afraid that would be the only way to save himself—if indeed he lived long enough to put the ring on some woman's finger.

Every instinct in him rebelled against being forced into marriage by anyone so unscrupulous and despicable as his cousin.

He turned from the window:

"What the devil am I to do, Watson?" he asked.

"I do not know, Your Grace, and that's the truth," Mr. Watson replied.

He hesitated before he continued:

"You can hardly lay an accusation against Mr. Giles when we have only flimsy circumstantial evidence against him. At the same time, I intend, with Your Grace's permission, to alert everyone with any authority on the estate."

He realised that the Duke was about to protest and he went on quickly:

"I shall, of course, say that the criminal is probably an escaped lunatic from Bedlam, or perhaps an Anarchist who has failed to assassinate the Queen and is now trying again a little lower down the Heraldic scale!"

The Duke laughed, but there was not much humour in the sound.

"Have it your own way, Watson. But I resent having to be on my guard against one of my own kith-and-kin, disreputable though he may be."

The Duke spoke violently and, as if to divert his attention to another topic, Mr. Watson said:

"Your Grace has received, this morning, a letter from the Bishop."

The Duke glanced at the pile of letters on his desk and said:

"I have not read them yet. What does he say?"

"The Bishop says, Your Grace, that he has exactly the right incumbent for the parish. He is the son of a Colonel Henderson, who served with you in the Regiment."

"I remember Henderson," the Duke said, "a charming man—and well-born. His wife, I think I am right in saying, is the daughter of Lord Lambert."

"That is correct, Your Grace."

"I will certainly welcome their son," the Duke said. "When is he calling to see me?"

"The Bishop states, Your Grace, that—if it would not inconvenience you—he would like you to see the Reverend John Henderson as quickly as possible."

"Why such haste?"

"He and his wife have to leave the house they have been occupying on a private estate because the Landowner's third son has just been ordained and wishes to be appointed to his father's parish."

The Duke nodded to show he understood that it was quite a usual procedure.

Then, as he sat down at his desk, he realised that Mr. Watson was waiting and—before he spoke—the Duke anticipated what he would say.

"That leaves us, Your Grace, with the problem of Miss Linton."

The Duke was still.

There was an uncomfortable silence until he said:

"If I thought it necessary, I would build a small house for Miss Linton."

"That will take time, Your Grace."

The Duke looked at his Secretary and knew he could read his thoughts.

"What you are saying, Watson, is . . ."

Before he could complete the sentence, the door of the Study opened and Selma came in.

She was looking extraordinarily attractive in a simple gown of leaf-green muslin which was swept back into a small bustle.

The colour accentuated the gold of her hair and the elfin look which always surprised the Duke every time he looked at her.

He thought now that she might have just come from the woods or the stream and was a nymph rather than a human being.

She moved towards the desk eagerly and her eyes seemed to light up as she said:

"I had to come to tell Your Grace that Daws and I have just removed the bandages and Mr. Oliver's skin is healing well."

She drew in her breath as if she were excited as she went on:

"It is, of course, very delicate and he must move as little as possible, but his ankle has set and we have been able to take off the splint."

The Duke was listening with a smile.

"This is certainly good news, Miss Linton."

"I felt you had to know at once," Selma said, "and Mr. Oliver wants to see you."

She paused and there was definitely a mischievous look in her eyes as she added:

"Of course, if Your Grace still wishes the Doctor to treat him, I hear that he returned to the Village last night."

The Duke laughed.

"You know perfectly well, Miss Linton," he said,

57

"that I am very satisfied with the progress my nephew has made under your skilful care."

He paused and then added:

"Although I am not yet prepared to acknowledge that you are a witch!"

It was now Selma who laughed.

"Real witches have all the fun," she said. "They go riding on broomsticks, visit the moon, and, of course, dance with the Devil in the woods at night!"

"Is that what you want to do?" the Duke enquired.

"I am more than content to go driving in a magical chariot," she replied.

She gave the Duke a questioning glance before she said:

"I have an urgent message from one of Your Grace's farms where a farm-boy has been gored by a bull. I have no way of reaching the farm, except on horseback."

She thought the Duke looked surprised and said:

"I can, of course, ride there, but I could not then take all the herbs that are required with me."

She paused and then explained:

"They are already prepared in bottles and these might get broken on the journey."

"Therefore, of course, under the circumstances it is my duty to take you to the farm," the Duke said.

Selma made a gesture with her hands before she said quickly:

"No . . . of course not . . . Your Grace! I did not . . . mean that. If I could . . . borrow one of your vehicles . . . I would be very . . . grateful."

"I will take you," the Duke said firmly.

He looked at the clock on the mantelpiece and said:

"We will have luncheon, Watson, in half an hour. Order my Phaeton for one-thirty."

"Very good, Your Grace," Mr. Watson replied.

He turned towards the door and then stopped.

"Shall I arrange for Your Grace to see the Reverend John Henderson tomorrow morning?"

There was silence while he knew the Duke battled with himself before he said reluctantly:

"Yes, Watson, and arrange—if he is satisfactory—to have all the furniture from the Vicarage transported to the Dovecote."

As he spoke, he was looking at Selma.

It seemed that her eyes opened so wide that they doubled in size before she exclaimed:

"The Dovecote! Are you . . . really letting . . . me go there? I . . . never . . . dreamt that you would . . . agree although . . . Mr. Hunter did . . . suggest it."

"I have no choice," the Duke said, "as there is no-where else and the Bishop has found an extremely suitable man to take over the parish."

Mr. Watson did not wait to hear any more and went from the Study, closing the door behind him.

There was silence and then Selma said in a small, hesitant voice:

"It is very . . . kind of . . . you, but I . . . know that you do not . . . want me to have . . . the Dovecote . . . so it would be . . . best if I went . . . away."

The Duke looked at her sharply as he thought she was merely pretending.

But there was no doubting the sincerity in her voice, and the expression in her eyes could not be misconstrued.

"Are you really prepared to leave the Village?" he asked.

"It would make me . . . very unhappy," Selma said honestly, "and I know that my grandfather does not want me. But . . . as there is nowhere for me to stay here . . . I shall . . . have to go to Scotland."

As she finished speaking, she turned away as if to leave the room and the Duke thought perhaps also to hide her tears.

He let her reach the door before he said:

"If you go, what are we to do about Oliver?"

Selma stopped and then turned back towards him very slowly.

"He is on the mend," she said after a moment, "and if he is very careful and does exactly what he is told, he should be able to walk in about two weeks."

"What about your other patients?"

Selma made a helpless gesture which was more explicit than words.

Then, as she put out her hand towards the door, the Duke said:

"As the Village cannot do without you, and you were certainly essential to my nephew, you will move into the Dovecote and there will be no more arguments about it."

She did not reply, but he sensed there was a certain tension about her.

It told him without words that it was what she wanted above all else.

Yet she was still disturbed by his aversion to her occupying what had always been a family house.

There was silence as she turned back and walked back towards him.

Selma stood facing him across the desk as she said:

"It is very kind of you, but I know what . . . your feelings . . . are."

She paused and then continued:

"What I would suggest, if Your Grace would agree, is that I move into the Dovecote until a cottage is available in the Village."

She looked away from him as she said:

"I think there is one . . . if not two . . . of the older pensioners who will not live . . . very long."

"Are you really suggesting," the Duke asked, "that you would be happy in one of those very small cottages which, I believe, consist of only three rooms?"

As he spoke he was quite convinced in his own mind that Selma was only pretending to be reluctant to take the Dovecote.

He was certain that she had intended to live there the moment her father died.

To his surprise she replied, in a practical tone:

"That is my problem, Your Grace."

She paused and then continued:

"I am sure that, as the cottages are very small, I could, if Your Grace allowed it, persuade some of the men in the Village to build on a small extension."

As if the Duke could read her thoughts, he could see that she was already planning how it could be done.

She was obviously quite sure that, because the Village wanted her so much, the men would do it willingly in their free time.

What was more, they would doubtless charge little or nothing for their labour.

She was looking so lovely and, at the same time, so ethereal that he knew no-one would grace the Dovecote better.

In fact, if he was honest, no-one could be more worthy of it.

Aloud he said:

"I do not like my arrangements being changed or questioned, Miss Linton, and you must therefore allow me to do things in my own way."

She looked at him as if she did not understand, and he went on:

"Your belongings will be moved, I am sure with the greatest care, into the Dovecote. You must instruct the men how to hang the curtains and what is to be put in each room."

He paused and then added:

"I hope you will be very happy there."

He saw a little tremor pass through Selma, and she clasped her hands together before she said simply:

"I know I shall be happy there and because there is the Herb Garden . . . which meant so much . . . to Mama I . . . shall not be . . . alone."

She added softly:

"Thank you. Thank you very much, Your Grace. Now will you please come to see Mr. Oliver."

As they went from the room, the Duke had the feeling that one of them—although he was not sure which —had won a notable victory.

*   *   *

Oliver was sitting up in bed and, although he looked rather pale, he was very much like his usual self and was surprisingly cheerful.

"Hello, Uncle Wade," he said as the Duke came into the room. "I shall soon be back in the saddle."

"That is what I wanted to hear," the Duke said. "Miss Linton has told me the good news."

"I have also been hearing the bad," Oliver said. "For Heaven's sake, Uncle Wade, be careful of Giles. He is determined to kill you."

"You cannot be absolutely sure of that," the Duke said lightly. "I am quite sure Giles would not risk his neck by murdering me obviously."

"Of course he would not do it obviously," Oliver answered. "But if you are found dead in the woods, or drowned in the lake, who would be able to say it was he who did it?"

Selma gave a little cry:

"There are so many ways he could kill you! You must be very, very careful."

The Duke sat down in an armchair.

"That is very easy to say," he said, "but what do you really expect me to do? Shut myself up in the house and never go out?"

He paused and then added:

"Or leave the country for the Far East, where Giles will not be able to follow me?"

"I think the best thing," Selma said, "is for everyone who loves you to be on their guard and also to . . . pray."

As if he felt he must argue with her, the Duke said:

"You really think that prayers can stop a statue falling on my head, or a bullet entering my back?"

He was teasing, but Selma answered quite seriously:

"I believe because you are good, while your cousin is bad, that God will protect you."

* * *

The next morning the Duke interviewed the Reverend John Henderson and found him to be an excellent and enthusiastic man.

He was, the Duke thought, just the type of Vicar that was wanted in the Village.

As soon as the Cleric and his wife had left, the Duke mounted his horse, which was waiting at the door, and set off across the Park.

It had infuriated him as he came down the front steps that he instinctively moved a little to one side instead of down the centre, as he usually did.

His brain told him that Giles would not try the same trick twice, of toppling a statue on his head.

But every instinct in his body reacted towards being cautious.

Mr. Hunter had sent the stonemasons up onto the roof and they had confirmed that the statue had been deliberately cut off its pedestal.

There was no possible way it would have fallen otherwise.

Mr. Watson had, in fact, advised the Duke not to ride alone.

The Duke had said firmly that he was too old to have a Nanny with him.

How ever many escorts he had, he could still be shot at, if that was to be Giles's next way of eliminating him.

He sounded brave but he knew, in the back of his mind, as he rode across the Park that he was being menaced, and it enraged him to know that he was so vulnerable.

He galloped his horse over a flat piece of land where there were no rabbit-holes.

He then turned to ride through one of his favourite woods, which led him to the Dovecote.

It was a lovely day with a promise of heat later in the afternoon.

The Duke was feeling particularly well and, despite his annoyance over his cousin, enjoying being in the country.

He knew that from a social point of view he should return to London.

Every day Mr. Watson informed him of more invitations from the Prince of Wales, the Prime Minister, and the many hostesses with whom he was *persona grata*.

They were bewildered by his disappearance at a time when as far as they were concerned, everything of importance was happening.

The Duke, however, knew he was far too busy with Oliver and, of course, Selma, to regret missing the huge Balls, the overcrowded Receptions, and gigantic dinners.

At the latter, he thought, everyone ate and drank far too much.

Because he was taking so much exercise, Daws had informed him only this morning when he was dressing that he had lost weight.

"If you goes on like this, Your Grace," Daws said, "you'll have to visit your Tailor, and you know that's somethin' which Your Grace doesn't enjoy."

"I would rather have my clothes taken in than let out," the Duke replied.

"No fear o'that, Your Grace!" Daws remarked, who always had to have the last word.

The Duke intended to see that Selma's furniture was being properly moved from the Vicarage to the Dovecote.

Mr. Watson had been so certain that the Reverend

John Henderson was exactly the Vicar they required that he had ordered Selma's furniture to be moved early that morning.

*   *   *

Almost before Selma had woken up, there was a rumble of wheels outside.

Nanny had come upstairs to tell her that there were a dozen men filling up their wagons with furniture from the downstairs rooms.

"Very nice they're being about it, too," Nanny said approvingly. "As they're doing it for you, dearie, they're handling everything as if it were made of china."

Selma laughed and got up hastily.

She had been told late the previous night what was happening and had arranged with Daws that he would look after Oliver this morning and she would call in the afternoon.

His foot, having been re-bandaged yesterday, meant there was really nothing important to be done but to keep him quiet.

Because he was feeling so much better, the difficulty was to prevent him from getting out of bed.

It did not take Selma long to pack a few things in her bedroom which required careful handling.

She was aware that what was in the drawers and wardrobes could be carried just as they were.

It was only a matter of going less than a mile to the Dovecote.

She was, in fact, very excited.

She would live in a house which she had always loved and which she felt had an atmosphere which was different from that of any other in the neighbourhood.

If there were ghosts in the past, they were soft, gentle, and loving ones.

She felt, too, that, because every occupant of the Dovecote had tended the Herb Garden, she and they would talk the same language.

*   *   *

As the first three wagons rumbled out of the driveway, Selma said "Goodbye" to the house which had been her home all her life.

She was not really sad at leaving because she felt that as she was going to the Dovecote, her father and mother came with her.

She could almost see them smiling and telling her how lucky she was and that was where they wanted her to be.

*   *   *

Selma rode over to the Dovecote on the horse which had carried her father for many years.

The horse was getting old and went there at a slow pace, so she found herself thinking and praying for the Duke.

She was terribly afraid that he might be injured.

She knew that the story of what happened had run through the Village like wildfire.

Everyone was deeply concerned at what they knew had been an attempt on the Duke's life.

It was only the fact that he had walked through the house to a side door much earlier to pick up his Phaeton in the Stables that had saved him.

Also a lucky chance had saved Mr. Oliver when he emerged from the front-door and had been mistaken for his uncle.

"How could this happen at Mortlyn of all places?" Selma asked herself.

Everything had always been so quiet and uneventful.

The great house had stood like a benign Palace, helping and protecting those beneath it.

Now suddenly they were all upset and apprehensive and there appeared to be no easy solution.

"How could this go on for years?" Selma asked herself, and there was no answer.

* * *

In the Dovecote the men unloaded quickly what they had brought in the wagons.

They were laying the carpets and hanging the curtains to Selma's satisfaction.

It was not difficult, as the rooms were more or less the same number and same size.

The Dovecote was more beautiful and certainly more ancient than the Vicarage.

Selma loved the diamond-paned casement windows, the polished floors, the dark beams and—most of all— the garden.

This had been kept in perfect condition not only because the Duke had ordered it, but because the gardeners, all of whom she knew well, wanted to please her.

Without being instructed, they would often plant new azaleas, rhododendrons, or other shrubs.

The Rose Garden had a number of rose trees which had, when they had been bought, been intended for the much bigger and more impressive display at Mortlyn.

"Oi knows ye'd want one of them pink roses which have just come from th' Botanical Garden, Miss," the Head Gardener would say.

He was well-rewarded when Selma smiled at him.

She always told him how much she appreciated the beauty of the Rose Garden which she went through every day when she tended her herbs.

There was no-one in the Village for whom the Herb

Garden was not a magical place which healed them when they were sick.

It also helped those who were old and were becoming senile.

"What ye gives me father 'as made 'im ten years younger, Miss," they would say to Selma, as they had said to her mother.

The old people seemed never to die, but were ready to care for their children, grandchildren, and great-grandchildren, long after their contemporaries in other Villages had passed away.

When the men had unloaded their wagons and gone back to the Vicarage for more, Selma moved instinctively towards the Herb Garden.

She was thinking before she reached it that when she was living in the Dovecote she would have the fountain turned on.

Then, as she went through the opening in the red brick wall she saw that one of the gardeners had anticipated her wishes and it was already playing.

She gave a little cry of delight and ran to where the cornucopia in the hand of Eros was throwing the water high into the air.

It caught the sunshine and fell down in a cascade of tiny rainbows into the carved stone basin.

It was so lovely that Selma, with her head thrown back, was staring up enraptured as the Duke came into the garden.

He stood still and it was impossible for him not to appreciate the picture she made.

The fountain was behind her so that she appeared to be almost inside the falling water.

The sunshine turned her hair to gold and it was difficult for the moment to think of her as an ordinary human being.

Rather was she part of the fountain, the gardens, and the strange fragrance of the herbs which he had noticed before.

Then, as if perceptively she was aware of him, she turned her head and, when she saw he was there, ran down the paved path towards him.

"Thank you...thank...you," she said in a rapt voice he had never heard from her before, "for letting me come...here."

She paused breathlessly and then went on:

"It is...so...so...beautiful! It is so...perfect! I have no words to tell you...what it...means to...me."

"You seem to belong here," the Duke said as if he could not help himself.

He looked round the garden and said:

"I thought I was fairly knowledgeable, but I realise now that I am very ignorant where herbs are concerned."

"Let me show you some of the very precious ones," Selma suggested.

She took him down one of the little paths, with its tiny clipped hedge.

They stopped and he listened as Selma pointed out Butcher's Brown, which was used for headaches, Cardius Benedictus, for the memory, and All Heal, for cramp.

The Duke was surprised to see a bed of Lilies of the Valley.

"Surely," he said, "these, at any rate, are for pleasure."

Selma laughed.

"Lilies of the Valley," she said, "have been used medicinally from the earliest times. They help the heart, eliminate the poison which causes inflammation in rheumatic diseases, and can also be used as a stimulant for the brain."

"I do not believe it," the Duke said, but he was smiling.

He thought as he spoke that Selma herself looked very much like a Lily of the Valley.

Then he said:

"I think, when you have finished moving into the Dovecote, you should come up to the house."

He paused and then went on:

"I know you want to see Oliver, and I also have some books in the Library which I think will interest you."

Selma looked at him and said:

"I would like that. I would love to see them. Are they about herbs?"

"They are books I never realised I had till now," the Duke said. "They are very old and were written at the time of Culpeper, about whom I now know quite a lot!"

Selma smiled.

She had not expected him to be interested in Nicholas Culpeper, who was the famous Astrologer Physician of the Seventeenth Century.

Then she was sure that the Duke disliked admitting his ignorance of anything, even if it concerned healing.

* * *

After the Duke had left her, Selma went home to supervise the arrival of the wagons filled with the bedroom furniture.

She found that on Mr. Watson's instructions two women from the Village had come in to clean the house.

They got the stove working in the kitchen, unpacked the china which had been put in crates, and did anything Nanny asked of them.

Selma was so touched at the kindness she had received.

She thought that everything had turned out so differently from her fear that she might have to leave the Village unless accommodation could be found for her.

Although Mr. Hunter had suggested the Dovecote, she had been quite certain that the Duke would not think her a suitable tenant.

That meant she would have to squeeze everything, including Nanny, into a tiny cottage if there was one.

The only alternative, which frightened her very much, was to journey to Scotland to her grandfather.

She had always been afraid of her mother's family, who had been so horrified that she had married an Englishman and left them to live in the South.

She knew it would be very hard if she had to be somewhere where her father was despised or abused in her hearing.

"I am so grateful . . . so very . . . very . . . grateful," Selma told herself as she looked round the Dovecote.

'I can live here,' she thought, 'and feel Mama is near me as I go on helping the people in the Village.'

She knew they needed her. She knew they loved and trusted her.

If she went away, she would always feel she had betrayed them.

*   *   *

Her heart was singing as, later in the afternoon, she rode towards the Big House.

Every time she looked at it it gave her a little thrill because it was so beautiful.

She wanted to look and to go on looking at something which, since she was very small, had meant stability and protection.

She drew her horse to a standstill under an old oak tree.

She looked at the lake, with the swans moving on its silver surface, and the patches of colour in the garden.

The Duke's Standard was flying on the roof of the house, showing that he was in residence.

As she looked at it she saw the empty place from which the statue had been pushed over and felt herself shiver.

Almost as though there was a voice telling her so,

71

she was suddenly aware that the Duke was once again in deadly danger.

At any moment his enemy might strike again.

Almost unconsciously she looked round as if expecting men with guns to be hiding behind the tree trunks, among the irises down by the lake, or in the bushes at the far end of it.

She looked back towards the woods which reached from the Dovecote towards the end of the lake.

Then bordering an Orchard, they joined the thick fir trees behind the house.

It was a wood she had always loved because it contained so many birch trees.

They made her think of the fairies and wood-nymphs by which she had been entranced as a child.

It was also because the ride through the centre of it was one of the prettiest and the most romantic on the whole estate.

It was then that Selma thought she caught a fleeting glimpse of a man moving amongst the trees.

It was just a quick impression, then he was gone and she thought she must have been mistaken.

It was very easy to imagine in the sunlight, and with a light wind moving the leaves, that she had seen what was not there.

She stared and went on staring but there was no further sign of anyone at all.

Selma told herself that she was just being imaginative.

Yet as she rode on towards the house, she knew she was afraid for the Duke.

It was a fear which seemed to streak through her and it was different from anything which she had ever felt before.

He was so magnificent, so dominating, so overwhelming, that it was impossible to think that he could be brought down treacherously.

It would be as if one of the great oak trees which had

stood there for hundreds of years had been felled.

Then, as she rode on, in the same way as she felt someone was telling her what to do when she treated a wound or an injury, she knew that the Duke was not only in danger but that it was coming nearer and still nearer to him.

She could feel it perceptively and, as her father would have called it, instinctively.

Although she had no proof, she knew that what she felt was true.

Somehow, although she had no idea how, she must save the Duke.

'How can . . . I? What . . . can I say? What can . . . I do?' she asked.

She was frightened by her conviction that she was not just imagining what she felt.

* * *

She reached the front-door and a Groom, who had been watching her come over the bridge which spanned the lake, was waiting to take her horse.

"Oi'll rub 'im down, Miss, an' give 'im somethin' to eat," the Groom said eagerly as if he wished to please her.

"That would be very kind, Sam," Selma replied. "Rufus is getting old, but he is still very nice to ride. I could not get here without him."

"Ye should get 'Is Grace to let ye ride one o' 'is new 'orses," Sam said. "They be fine . . . th' finest we've ever 'ad."

"His Grace has been very kind to me already," Selma said, "by letting me move into the Dovecote."

"That be th' right place for ye, Miss, us all be a-thinkin' that."

Selma took down a bundle of herbs which she had attached to the pommel of her saddle.

"These are for Mr. Oliver," she said. "He will soon be riding His Grace's horses."

"An' all due to ye, Miss," Sam said as he led her horse away.

Selma smiled as she entered the Hall and went up the Grand Staircase to the first floor.

She then became serious, because she was feeling again that awesome conviction that the Duke was in danger.

She wondered how she could tell him to be more careful than he was being already.

She knew that Mr. Watson, Graves, and practically everyone in the house would have warned him a hundred times that Giles Lyne was dangerous.

However, she knew that what she was feeling was different from their obvious concern.

What she had received was a message.

A message from God or perhaps the Power that she believed helped her heal those that were sick.

A Power that was so real that she could not only feel it vibrating through her but sometimes even see it.

A light would envelop a patient and that was always a sign from the Divine.

'I must tell him, and I must save him,' Selma thought as she walked along the corridor.

Then almost frantically the question came from the very depths of her being:

'How can I do it? What can I say? How can I make him believe me?'

She reached Oliver's room and, as she did so, Daws opened the door.

"Ah, there you are, Miss Selma!" he exclaimed. "Mr. Oliver has been asking for you—he thinks you had forgotten him."

"You know I would never do that. How is he?" Selma asked.

She spoke in a low voice so that their patient would not hear.

"Bored, Miss," Daws replied. "That's the only thing wrong with him. He wants you to cheer him up."

"I will do my best," Selma replied.

Daws opened the door wide and she went into the bedroom.

Oliver was sitting up, with books and newspapers strewn in front of him.

As she appeared he said:

"Here you are at last. I thought you had forgotten me."

"You know I would not do that."

"How do I know it?" Oliver asked petulantly. "You may have half a dozen young men fawning on you in the Village, or perhaps, like all the stupid women in London, you are in love with Uncle Wade."

Selma looked at him, her eyes twinkling and with a smile on her lips.

Then as she was about to tell him that he was talking nonsense, she knew it was the truth.

Of course she was in love with the Duke!

That was why she was not only afraid for him but also more pulsatingly aware than anyone else how close to him the danger was.

chapter four

SELMA found herself unable to sleep.

It had all been so exciting!

She had talked for a long time to Oliver and had left him far more cheerful as a result of her visit.

Then the Duke had suggested that she come to the Library.

He wanted her to see the books about which he had told her.

She found them fascinating because they included a first Edition of Nicholas Culpeper's Complete Herbal.

She handled it, the Duke thought as he watched her, with the reverence with which a Moslem would handle his Koran, or a Christian the Bible.

She opened the Herbal and found some of the herbs mentioned which she had shown him in the garden of the Dovecote.

She read aloud in her musical voice the words that Culpeper had written in the Seventeenth Century.

She also told the Duke how he had been married and became the father of seven children.

During the Civil War he had fought on the Parliamentary side against King Charles and had been wounded in the chest.

"He was obviously what we would call 'a Revolutionary,'" the Duke said to tease her. "I expect, as you admire him so much, you, too, would wish to oppose the Monarchy!"

"How could you think anything so wrong about me!" Selma exclaimed.

Then she realised that the Duke was deliberately trying to provoke her and she laughed.

"I believe in Kings and Queens," she said, "and especially Charles II."

"All women love a Rake," the Duke remarked cynically.

"I do not admire him for that," Selma replied, "but because he had such excellent taste and was the first to introduce ducks into St. James's Park."

The Duke looked surprised.

"Did he do that?"

"Of course he did—their descendants are there today, but I do not suppose the people of London are interested in anything so countrified."

"I am interested," the Duke said. "I hope you admire my swans."

"I think they are lovely, very romantic, and exactly what you should have at Mortlyn."

"Thank you," he replied, "and I suppose you think, having said that, that Mortlyn itself is romantic."

Selma longed to tell him that not only the house but the owner of it were part of her secret dreams.

Then she was terrified that the Duke would think that she was running after him, as, according to Oliver, all the women in London were doing.

"Mortlyn does not seem real," she said lightly, "and that is why nothing should spoil it in any way."

The Duke knew that she was thinking of Giles trying to kill him, and, he thought, if anything was unreal, it was Selma herself.

He remembered how she had looked against the fountain in the Herb Garden.

They went on talking about books and the Duke produced some beautiful drawings by famous artists, which he said he had had no idea he possessed until then.

Selma was delighted with them and, when she was poring over them, exclaiming that each one was more beautiful than the last, the Duke said unexpectedly:

"I think you should be painted and I am wondering who would do you justice. It is a pity there is no Joshua Reynolds or Boucher today."

He did not expect Selma to be conversant with either of these artists, but she smiled and said:

"Now you really are flattering me! Papa always longed for Mama to be painted, but he said that only Sir Joshua Reynolds, who had been dead for fifty years, would have captured her beauty on canvas."

She smiled and added:

"Or else he would have wished Fragonard to be available."

The Duke was surprised but he did not say anything.

He merely took Selma along the corridor and into a room which was seldom used.

Over the mantelpiece there was a delightful picture by Boucher of the goddess Diana resting after the exertions of the chase.

It was so lovely that Selma gave a cry of excitement and clapped her hands together.

The Duke was looking from the goddess to Selma.

He decided that, if it were a question of a second judgement of Paris and his awarding a golden apple to the fairer of the two, he would give it to Selma.

And yet, he told himself that she was not a conventional beauty.

The elfin look about her would be hard to convey in oils.

Then, as if he thought that it was a mistake to flatter her, he took her to the front door, where her horse was waiting.

As it was such a short way from the Dovecote to the Big House, Selma had not changed into riding-clothes.

She sprang into her saddle wearing the cotton dress she had put on first thing in the morning.

She realised now for the first time, and was embarrassed by the discovery, that she had also forgotten to wear a bonnet.

She was so used to running into the Village quite informally from the Vicarage or visiting the Park and the woods that she seldom "dressed up."

The exception being when she had first visited the Duke.

Now, as he lifted her into the saddle, she said a little shyly:

"I must apologise if I look unconventional, but the men were still arranging the furniture in my bedroom when I left."

"You look exactly right to be the *Chatelaine* of the Dovecote," the Duke replied.

He saw an expression of delight in Selma's eyes and, after she had left, he walked slowly back into the house.

He told himself that it would be a great mistake for him to become too much involved with the girl.

After all, it would be disastrous if she fell in love with him, which his experience told him she was quite likely to do.

The sooner he went back to London, to the women with whom he usually spent his time, the better.

Then he remembered that he was bored with Doreen Bramwell.

There had been a whole succession of other Beauties also who had held his interest for a few weeks—occasionally a few months.

Yet invariably, sooner than he expected, they made him yawn.

So far he had not yawned with Selma, although she was, of course, in a very different category from the women he knew in London.

If he were honest, he would have admitted that she interested and intrigued him.

Whatever she said was unexpected.

He told himself that although she was very young, she had a composure and a serenity which was seldom found except in very much older women.

As he walked upstairs towards Oliver's room, he found himself wondering what Selma's future would be.

After all, whatever she might say, she could hardly contemplate living for the rest of her life in the Dovecote.

She would have only her old Nurse as a companion and she would spend her days tending to the villagers' ailments.

She was not likely to meet many eligible men in Little Mortlyn.

Then it struck him that the only marriageable men she could meet would be those he entertained when he came to the country.

He tried to imagine how she would fit into any of the parties which he gave in his house in London, and those he intended to give at Mortlyn.

He had the unmistakable feeling that even though they were luxuriously dressed and glittering with jewels, his women friends would be eclipsed by Selma.

Then he told himself that he was being ridiculous.

How could the Vicar's daughter, however well-bred, compete with the sophisticated and witty Beauties who enthralled the Prince of Wales, or any of the other men who were his fellow members at White's.

The whole idea was laughable.

Then, as he walked along the corridor, it occurred to him that just as Selma intrigued him, she would attract his contemporaries.

They would find her, as he had, unusual, interesting, and intriguing.

Strangely enough, the idea annoyed him. As he opened Oliver's door, he said beneath his breath:

"The sooner I get back to London, the better."

But even as he walked towards his nephew, who was

obviously delighted to see him, the Duke was aware that he did not want to leave Mortlyn.

* * *

To Selma, the Duke's kindness in showing her his books and talking about his pictures was something she wanted to remember.

She would also treasure it in her heart.

She knew she would think of him not only now, when there was a chance of seeing him again, but after he was gone and she was alone in the Dovecote.

She was aware that he would fill her thoughts and she would pray ceaselessly for his safety.

However, he must never know how much she thought of him, or how much she loved him.

'I shall see him today!' she told herself when she awoke.

Because the idea was so exciting, Selma jumped out of bed, washed in cold water, and started to dress.

It was too early for Nanny to be about, and she thought she would go to the Herb Garden.

Then she had another idea.

She had not forgotten how, on her way to the Big House, she had been vividly aware that the Duke was in danger.

Before going to sleep, she had remembered again the man she thought she had seen in the wood.

'It was just my imagination,' she decided, but the presentiment of danger was still there.

Now, as it came back to her, she remembered that theRide through the wood led to the flat ground where the Duke exercised his horses.

It suddenly struck her that if he went there this morning, as he was very likely to do, the man she had seen might be waiting for him.

He could shoot him down and then escape through the trees before he was seen.

The mere idea made her feel as if an icy hand clutched at her heart.

Selma let herself out of the house. Everything was very quiet as she went towards the stables.

The dew was still on the grass, there was a mist round the foot of the trees, and she knew it would be hanging over the lake until it was dispersed by the sun.

The world smelt young and very fresh.

She could hear the birds singing in the trees. If they were unafraid, there could be no danger, she told herself.

And yet the same feeling as she had had yesterday made her saddle old Rufus and draw him out of his stall into the yard.

There was no sign of Ted, the man who not only looked after Rufus but also stoked the boiler at the Vicarage.

He planted the vegetables in the garden and even gave Nanny a hand in the Kitchen if she was overworked.

Ted had been more pleased than anyone when Selma had told him that she was moving into the Dovecote.

"Now that's th' right place for ye, Miss Selma," he said with satisfaction. "Th' garden be in fine shape so Oi won't have so much t' do outside."

"What I want, if I can ever afford it," Selma said, "is to buy another horse. I would never part with Rufus, but he is getting rather old."

"Ye try an' borrow one o' 'em 'orses from 'Is Grace's stable," Ted replied. "That's be cheaper than spendin' yer own money."

Selma laughed because Ted always had such practical ideas.

But as she mounted Rufus, she told herself that she must be very careful not to impose on the Duke.

After he had granted her the Dovecote to live in, she must not let him think that, like Oliver Twist, she was asking for more.

"He has been so kind . . . so wonderful," she whispered to herself.

She felt as if the rays of the sun coming up over the horizon were seeping into her body at the thought of him.

Then she remembered that he might be in danger.

She forced Rufus to move a little quicker into the wood, where it ended at one of the brick walls surrounding the garden.

First there was only a narrow path, twisting and turning between the trees.

After she had ridden for about ten minutes, the wood expanded and she came to the beginning of the Ride, which was cut right through the centre of it.

In some places the branches of the trees, when they were in full leaf, met overhead and gave the impression of a tunnel.

The moss had grown on the path to make it soft for the horses' hooves.

The wood on either side had always seemed to Selma to be enchanted.

She pulled in Rufus for a moment to look towards the end of the Ride.

As she did so, she was almost sure she saw someone moving through the undergrowth under the trees.

Quickly she dismounted and, drawing Rufus off the path, she took him into the thickness of the wood.

There was no need to tie him up.

She knew if she let him loose, he would merely forage around for something to eat and wait for her return.

Moving very quietly, Selma picked up her skirts with both hands and moved through the trees towards where she thought she had seen the man.

Without thinking what she should wear that morning, she had put on the first dress she had found hanging in her wardrobe.

It was, in fact, her green muslin, which blended with the shrubs and made her almost invisible.

Because, since she was a child, she had watched the rabbits playing, the deer resting under the oaks, and the birds feeding their young, she could move as silently as any native Indian.

Perhaps because she loved them, birds did not take flight, nor did animals scuttle away at her approach.

Selma moved forward steadily but not too quickly because that might have betrayed her presence.

Then, as she heard a voice, she stood still.

She had not walked along the side of the Ride but deeper in the wood.

Now she was aware that, as she stopped behind the trunk of the great elm, the voice she had heard came from the Ride, which was several yards to her right.

"'Ere'd be th' best plice, Bill," a man's voice said.

He had a strange accent which told Selma that he was not a local man.

"Oi'll 'ave ter move a bit 'igher," another man replied.

Selma was certain that he was on the approach side of the Ride.

"Be ye well 'idden?" the first man asked.

"Aye, there's a bush 'ere an' a tree Oi can get th' rope round."

"Cum on, 'urry oop," the first man said. "'E'll be a-comin' soon."

It was then, with a sense of horror, that Selma realised what the men—she was now aware they spoke with a Cockney accent—were doing.

They were putting a rope across the Ride.

When the Duke appeared as they expected, he would be galloping towards the flat ground which was not far ahead.

They would raise the rope at the last moment.

This would catch his horse just below the knees and he would stop dead, pitching his rider over his head.

It was an old trick, and Selma was well aware how successful it could be.

It was something which no unsuspecting rider could see until it was too late.

Selma knew that she must warn the Duke.

She turned round and started to move back as quickly as she dared in the direction from which she had come.

She knew he would enter the Ride from the Park about halfway down it and she must stop him before he reached the wood.

Then, as she was held up by brambles entangled in the skirt of her gown, she realised she was too late!

She heard the sound of a horse's hooves.

Because they had been softened in the distance by the moss and grass on the Ride, the Duke had passed where she was standing before she had even time to call out.

She could not scream but gave a choked cry seeing his head and shoulders as he galloped past.

As she held her breath she heard the Duke shout and the crash as his horse fell.

For a moment she felt she might faint from the sheer horror of it.

Then through the noise of the horse thrashing about and snorting in pain she could hear the voices of the two men.

One of them said:

"Mind them 'ooves, Bill, and 'it 'im 'ard!"

"'E mayn't be dead unless us 'it 'im," the other replied.

Selma realised she must do something and quickly.

Almost as if her father were helping and guiding her, she shouted out in her own voice:

"Ted! Ted! Come here quickly—there has been an accident!"

She moved forward as she did so, rustling the brushes. She could see the heads of the two men as they stood in the Ride.

She could also see that one of them held a bludgeon —a particularly unpleasant one which she thought had nails hammered into it to make it more deadly.

Lowering her tone of voice so that, except to anyone very discriminating, it would sound like a man's, Selma shouted:

"Oi be a-comin', Miss! Oi've the dogs with Oi! Ben an' Jim be just behind Oi."

It was quite a good imitation of the way Ted spoke.

Selma watched the men, particularly the one with the bludgeon, and knew they were indecisive.

"Come on, come on, quickly," she screamed. "Hurry, Ted, and shoot them before they escape."

"Oi'll blow their 'eads off their bodies, Miss," the supposed Ted shouted back. "'Urry, Jim, 'urry, us can't let 'em devils get away."

It was then that Selma heard one of the men say:

"What be we a-waitin' fur? They'll get us if us stay 'ere."

Bill, who was on Selma's side of the Ride, ran across it.

She saw two heads—one wearing a cap, the other a disreputable old hat—disappear among the trees.

Because she was afraid they might not go far, she kept up her shouts and made Ted say:

"'Ere, Jim, 'ere be 'Is Grace! One o' ye catch 'is 'orse."

She was sure, from the sounds the two men made running through the trees, that they had not stopped.

Only when she felt certain that they had left the wood did she run into the Ride to see what had happened.

The Duke's horse had struggled onto his feet.

His knees were cut and bleeding and the wretched animal was obviously in pain.

Ahead, lying face downwards on the Ride, was the still body of the Duke.

Selma rushed to his side and, kneeling down, felt him very gently.

She was praying that he had broken no more than his collar-bone, or perhaps his shoulder.

There was always the chance that in such an accident with such a large horse a man could break his neck by falling forwards onto his head.

It was difficult to know how badly injured he was.

She realised that he was unconscious and that she should get help.

It was then she saw the bludgeon with which one of the assailants had been going to attack the Duke.

As she had feared, it was a terrifying instrument which had two-inch nails driven into the head.

If the Duke had been struck with it, he would quite certainly now be dead.

She stood for a moment looking at it and listening, just in case the men were returning.

But everything was quiet—so quiet that she knew the birds had been frightened and had flown away.

The Duke's horse, a magnificent black stallion, was breathing heavily and trembling. Selma patted him.

Then, going to the Duke's side, she began to pull him as gently as she could off the Ride.

On one side there was a ditch which had been dug for drainage purposes, and was half filled with leaves.

She managed, with an almost superhuman effort, to drag the Duke slowly into the ditch.

There she covered him with the dead leaves which were in and around it.

Then she picked up the bludgeon and threw it as far as she could into the bushes at the other side of the Ride.

She thought, as she did so, how heavy it was.

Merely to touch it, knowing for what it had been intended, made her shiver.

Although it took time, she managed to remove the rope which had caused the stallion to fall.

She knew that, if the men returned, they would find it difficult to remember exactly where their evil booby-trap had been laid.

It was only when she was sure that the Duke would

not be found before she returned that she led the lame, bleeding, and frightened horse down the middle of the Ride.

They walked very slowly until she reached the place where she had left Rufus.

All the time she was thinking what she must do.

She was still very frightened but she felt as if she were being helped and guided by someone wiser than herself.

In a way it prevented her from feeling the full horror of what occurred.

Only when she had left the stallion and mounted Rufus to ride back to the Dovecote did she realise that tears were pouring down her cheeks.

Also she felt cold and faint while her whole body was trembling.

As she rode up to the front door of the Dovecote, to her utter relief she saw Mr. Hunter's trap coming down the drive.

Sitting beside him was his eldest son, a clever young man who was working with his father in the hope that he might become the agent on some gentleman's estate.

She knew then that luck was with her and the Duke.

It struck her, as she started to hail Mr. Hunter, that it would be a mistake to allow the men who had run away to know that their mission had failed.

* * *

It was nearly two hours later, when the Duke had been carried into the Dovecote and Nanny and Mr. Hunter had got him into bed, before they allowed Selma to examine him.

She went into the room to see him lying in the carved four-poster which had been her father's bed.

She thought that he was curiously pale and, for one terrifying moment, imagined that he might be dead.

It was Nanny who reassured her:

"His Grace's still unconscious, dearie, but his heart's beating. I knows you'll be able to help him."

"Yes, of course," Selma replied.

She managed to sound more confident than she actually was.

It was one thing to treat Oliver and the people she knew in the Village, but she loved the Duke.

That made her desperately afraid that she might fail him.

Then the Power which always poured through her when people came to her who were injured or in pain made her forget herself.

She knew what was wrong with him.

Very gently she examined his shoulder and his collar-bone, which were unbroken, and then the back of his neck.

This was where she had been most afraid of injury, but she found it was not as bad as it might have been.

The Power which directed her told her what to do and reassured her.

Although it would take time, she could, with the help of God, make the Duke whole again.

She knew, however, that when he did recover consciousness, he would suffer from severe concussion.

This would mean that the violence with which he had been thrown would give him blinding headaches.

Nanny and Mr. Hunter stood back from the bed whilst she examined the Duke and waited for her verdict.

"His Grace has damaged his spinal cord," Selma said in a low voice. "I can heal it, but it will take time."

She paused, then went on:

"If you will stay with him, Nanny, Mr. Hunter can come with me to get the herbs I need."

She went from the room and, when they were outside, she said to Mr. Hunter:

"I think it would be a great mistake that anyone, except perhaps Mr. Oliver, should know that the Duke is here and that he is alive."

Mr. Hunter looked surprised and Selma explained:

"His assailants were rough Cockneys from London. It would be wise to allow them to say when they report to the person who sent them that the Duke is dead."

She thought for a moment and then continued:

"That will at least give us breathing-space and allow us to get him better. On no account must he be disturbed or injured a second time."

Mr. Hunter understood what she was thinking.

If the Duke was at Mortlyn, it could be difficult to protect him there.

Moreover, if Giles Lyne was aware that his diabolical trap had not killed his cousin, he would be thinking up another method of doing so.

"I understand, Miss Selma," Mr. Hunter replied. "You can trust my son to keep his mouth shut, but I think we should get Daws to help you nurse His Grace."

"Yes, of course," Selma agreed. "I feel it is absolutely imperative for someone to be with him by day and by night."

"It would be a mistake for me to stay at the Dovecote," Mr. Hunter said. "It would arouse too much curiosity."

He paused and then continued:

"But my son, who is an excellent shot, can be on guard at night and the Village would merely think that he is away on business."

"That would be very helpful."

Selma walked across to the Herb Garden and picked the herbs she needed.

As she did so, she was praying that the Duke would soon be as strong as he had been the day he had found her at the fountain, the day when she had thanked him for allowing her to live at the Dovecote.

"I love him," she told the herbs as she picked them. "Make him well. Please, God, make him well."

When they went back to the house Mr. Hunter said that he was going to ride around the Park as if in the ordinary way of duty.

At the same time, he would be searching for any sign of the felons.

"If I do find them, Miss Selma," he said, "I don't mind telling you that I shall not hesitate to kill them both."

"I think you would be justified, Mr. Hunter," Selma replied, "but I doubt if they will linger when they think that their mission is completed."

*   *   *

Mr. Hunter had sent his son to find the Duke's stallion and bring him very slowly and gently to the Dovecote.

By this time he was in the stable, and Mr. Hunter and Selma went to see the poor animal.

Ted was there, washing and bandaging the stallion's knees.

"'E's 'ad a bad fall, Miss."

"I know," Selma replied, "but I do not want anyone to know about it. Please do not tell anyone in the Village that the horse is here."

She knew that Ted would obey her and he said:

"Oi knows when t' keep me mouth shut, Miss."

"I know you do, Ted, and that is why I am trusting you."

She left the three men talking about the horse and went back to the Duke. He had not moved since she left him.

She gave Nanny the herbs.

"Before I do the herbs," Nanny said, "I am going to get you something to drink, dearie. You look as pale as a ghost, and that's the truth."

"I am all right," Selma replied.

She knew that it was the shock which had swept the colour from her face.

However, she did not demur when Nanny hurried away to make her something warm and sweet, which was her unfailing palliative for shock, strain, or unhappiness.

When she had gone, Selma sat down beside the Duke and put her hand on his forehead.

He was cold, but it was not the coldness she had feared when she first saw him in bed.

"You must get well," she said very quietly beneath her breath.

She went on in her soft voice:

"You are so strong and so magnificent that it is an insult that such despicable people should make you . . . suffer or . . . fall from the . . . pedestal on which . . . we have all put . . . you."

She laid her hand over his. There were no longer the vivid vibrations which she had felt before whenever he touched her.

She knew he needed more strength than she could give him, and she began to pray.

She prayed that the Power and light in which she believed would pour down upon him and heal him.

As she went on praying, she felt as if the light were there.

Clear as a silver moonbeam high in the sky, it covered the Duke with its silver radiance, like the falling water of the fountain.

She felt it must bring the Duke the healing he needed and give him the strength to become his whole self again.

She prayed with an intensity which made her feel as if she reached up to Heaven itself.

When a little later the door opened and Nanny came in with her warm, sweet drink, she felt exhausted.

It was as if she had given the Duke her heart and her soul, and with them the life that flowed through her body.

"I have never heard anything more diabolical!" Oliver exclaimed when Selma told him what had happened to his uncle.

"I am going to get up," he said the next day, "to come and guard Uncle Wade myself."

He paused and then went on angrily:

"If those devils learn he is alive, they will be back. You can be sure of that. Giles wants money and he wants to be a Duke."

"I refuse to have two invalids on my hands," Selma protested.

"There is nothing wrong with me," Oliver answered, "except that I want to murder Giles. I am just thinking of the best way to do it."

Selma told him that he must be sensible.

* * *

Selma was not surprised when, two days later, Oliver arrived at the Dovecote and was carried into the house on a chair by two Footmen.

"I am missing all the fun," he said when Selma remonstrated with him.

By this time she had realised, as did Mr. Hunter, that they could no longer go on pretending that the Duke was dead.

He was alive but, as Selma had predicted, he had blinding headaches.

There was nothing she could do except give him herbs to relieve the pain.

At the same time, she knew that the massage she was giving him, which she had been taught by her mother, was very effective.

There was nothing broken in his spinal column, but it was badly jarred and bruised.

The flesh on his neck and shoulders was also tender and bruised.

She was confident, however, that his brain was undamaged.

When he regained consciousness, he confirmed this and was at the same time extremely disagreeable at being unable to move without pain.

He also found it, at times, hard to think clearly.

"You will have to be patient," Selma said as she massaged his neck and shoulders.

"That is one thing I have never been able to be," he replied. "I suppose you are thinking that it is very good for me to realise I am not as omnipotent as I thought I was."

Selma laughed.

"Of course that is what I am thinking and, as you say, it is very good for your soul."

"I do not believe I have one," the Duke said for the sake of argument.

"Actually," Selma replied, "it is in very good shape and, although you may deny it, is a very important part of your anatomy."

"I doubt if I could find a picture of it in any medical book."

"Well, I can tell you that as far as I am concerned, it wears a small halo on the top of its head."

Selma smiled, then continued:

"It inspires a great many people, including your nephew, Oliver, to do not only what is sporting but also what is right."

The Duke considered this for a moment and then he said as if he were embarrassed by the compliment she had paid him:

"Are you saying that Oliver is behaving himself?"

"Oliver is deeply concerned about you and is practising shooting every day from a wheel-chair so that if Giles tries to murder you again, he will be able to kill him first."

"Good Heavens!" the Duke ejaculated. "If he commits murder, he may find himself hanged whilst Giles gets off scot-free."

"I think that is unlikely," Selma said. "But it is good for Oliver to be thinking of someone other than himself."

The Duke was aware that Selma and his nephew had become very close in their anxiety for him.

It was Oliver who had said to her:

"Oh, for goodness' sake, stop calling me Mr. Oliver! It makes me sound like Methuselah. And I have no intention of calling you Miss Selma as if I was one of the servants."

Selma laughed:

"I see no reason why we should be so formal."

"It is something I have no intention of being," Oliver replied.

He paused and then went on:

"If I am related to Uncle Wade, so are you! You cluck over him as if you were a broody old hen with only one chick."

"If you were not an invalid, I would throw something at you," Selma exclaimed.

"And being a girl, you would miss!"

They had both laughed.

Selma thought what fun it was to have someone of her own age to play with—for that was what she and Oliver were doing.

The Duke noticed their growing intimacy.

It had struck him quite unexpectedly that if Oliver fell in love with Selma, it would be a very good thing.

It would certainly keep him away from the avaricious Cyprians.

The idea made him curious so that he could not resist saying to Selma when she was massaging him:

"Oliver is growing into a handsome young man. Are you in love with him?"

The question took Selma by surprise.

"No . . . of course . . . not," she said quickly. "I feel as if Oliver is the brother I never had. Being . . . in love is . . . very different."

"How do you know?" the Duke enquired.

Too late she realised that she had spoken too positively.

"I had the idea," he went on, "when I first met you, that you had never been in love with anyone and knew very little about it."

"That is . . . true."

"Well, then, how can you be sure that you are not in love with Oliver?"

There was a silence before Selma said:

"I am sure. But it is . . . something I . . . cannot put into . . . words."

"That surprises me," the Duke remarked. "I have always thought that you are remarkably articulate for someone who had never travelled from Mortlyn!"

Selma laughed.

"Now you are being rather foolish, which is unlike you."

She explained:

"With Papa's help I visited many parts of the world and, of course, again with his . . . help reached the . . . gates of . . . Heaven."

She realised as she spoke that that was what she had done when she prayed for the Duke.

She had felt that only by pleading with God would He send her all the help she needed to make the Duke well.

As if he could read her thoughts, the Duke asked:

"Have you been praying for me, Selma?"

"You must be aware," Selma answered after a moment's hesitation, "that you would not otherwise have . . . recovered as . . . well as you have. Your headaches are far better yesterday and today . . . than they were . . . before."

She waited for a moment and then continued:

"It is due to a Power which is far . . . far stronger than . . . anything which I alone can . . . do for . . . you."

"And yet the Power of which you speak," the Duke said, "comes through you to me. You are not going to deny that?"

Again there was a pause before Selma said in a low voice:

"I like to . . . think that is . . . true."

She wiped away the herbal oil which she had put on the Duke's neck and shoulders before she massaged him.

Then she helped him very gently to lie back against his pillows.

As she would have moved away from the bed, he caught her hand and held it.

"I want to look at you," he said. "I cannot believe you are real and not a figment of my imagination."

"Why should I . . . not be . . . myself?"

"It is almost impossible for anyone so young to be so intelligent and to know so many things that are not granted to other people. How could you acquire all that in eighteen years?"

She smiled and as if she had answered, he said:

"I know what you are going to say. It may be the Nineteenth Century, but you have already lived a thousand lives as a Healer, a Doctor, or—of course—a witch, before you became little Miss Selma."

"You make it sound very exciting." Selma smiled. "If you have nothing better to do when you return to Mortlyn, you might write a book."

"With you as the heroine?" the Duke enquired. "Who would be the hero?"

For one moment her eyes met his.

It was impossible for either of them to look away.

chapter five

THE previous day Selma had come down the stairs at Mortlyn having treated Oliver's leg.

Needless to say, he had been doing too much and she had to read him a strict lecture on being more careful.

"It is so boring here," Oliver complained. "If I was with you and Uncle Wade, it would be different."

"With the best will in the world," Selma laughed, "I do not think we can squeeze any more people into the Dovecote."

It was not a large house, and besides Nanny, there were Daws, Emily, Mr. Hunter's son, and a Footman all sleeping in the house.

The Chef, Amy, and the Footmen, who relieved each other both by night and day, arrived every morning and left late in the evening.

It made Selma laugh, when she thought that she and Nanny were going to be alone there, to realise that the small house was as busy as a bee-hive.

But she understood what Oliver meant, and she said:

"If you will just be patient for a little while, then you will be able to do everything you want."

She went on in a serious tone:

"The new skin which is growing on your leg is very, very delicate and, if you make it sore and uncomfortable, you will have only yourself to blame."

"Skin or no skin," Oliver said crossly, "I intend to go riding tomorrow."

"Very well," Selma agreed, "but please keep your leg up today and rest as much as you can. I cannot have two invalids on my hands."

"Two?" Oliver questioned. "Is Uncle Wade bad again?"

"He was impatient like you," Selma replied. "He not only got out of bed—which he was not supposed to do—but walked about until he brought on one of his blinding headaches."

"I thought you were supposed to prevent that from happening," Oliver teased.

"I gave him Chrysanthemum Leaves," Selma answered, "and this morning he is well again but very disagreeable."

"I had better come over and protect you from His Grace's rage," Oliver suggested.

"Tomorrow," Selma said firmly, "and you are to take it easy and try to sleep after luncheon."

"You are a bully—that is what you are!" Oliver protested.

Selma only laughed at him.

She realised, however, that it was a mistake to allow him to feel so depressed.

She thought she would suggest to the Duke that one or two people of Oliver's age should be invited to luncheon or dinner at Mortlyn.

It would amuse him to play the Host and she was sure the Duke would agree.

As she reached the Hall, she was thinking how kind he was about so many things and how much she loved him.

Then she was aware that Graves was opening the front door and that someone had just arrived in a carriage.

She moved away to stand underneath the staircase, thinking that it would be a mistake, if strangers were calling, for them to see her.

Then she heard Graves saying:

"Good day, Captain Seymour, it is nice to see you again."

"I have come," the newcomer answered, "to find out what has happened to His Grace. I found it very strange not to have heard from him."

"That is what I feel too!" a woman's voice exclaimed.

Selma had moved so far under the shadow of the staircase that she could not see who was speaking.

Now, because she was curious, she took a step forward and saw that facing Graves there was a tall, good-looking young man.

Besides him was one of the most beautiful women she had ever seen.

It was not only her face which was so arresting, but the way she was dressed.

She was wearing a very elegant travelling-bonnet ornamented with flowers and a veil. It was very different from anything which had ever appeared in Little Mortlyn.

The gentleman walked farther into the Hall, saying:

"Well, Graves, are you going to inform His Grace that we are here? Or send us back to London?"

"I have certainly no intention of going back," the lady said. "I already feel exhausted by the long drive."

Selma was aware that Graves was hesitating as to how to reply to all this and wondering whether he should reveal that the Duke was not at Mortlyn.

Feeling she should help him, Selma moved forward into the Hall and, walking towards the new arrivals, she said:

"I think I should explain that His Grace has had an accident."

"An accident?" the gentleman exclaimed. "Why was I not told?"

He looked at Graves as he spoke and Graves said apologetically:

"His Grace did not wish anyone in London to be

made anxious by learning what had happened to him."

"Are you staying here at Mortlyn?" the lady asked Selma.

There was a note in her voice which sounded as if she deeply suspected the whole situation.

Selma said hastily:

"My name is Selma Linton and, as I am skilled in nursing, I have been looking after Mr. Oliver, who also has had an accident."

"You certainly do not look to me like a Nurse," the lady said sharply.

The gentleman, however, was more pleasant.

"I think we must introduce ourselves. My name is Charles Seymour and I am a very old friend of the Duke's."

He smiled at her and continued:

"This is Lady Bramwell, who has travelled down with me from London because we were both so worried that something untoward had occurred."

"I think," Lady Bramwell said haughtily, "it is quite unnecessary for us to explain ourselves, Charles. Let us see Wade immediately and he can tell us what has happened."

She spoke in a tone which told Selma that she resented her presence.

Lady Bramwell had then turned away to move towards the Drawing Room, which was directly in front of where they were standing.

Selma looked at Graves and decided that there was nothing they could do but tell the truth.

She said in her soft voice:

"I am afraid that His Grace is not here. Mr. Oliver is upstairs, if you would like to see him."

"Not here?" Lady Bramwell exclaimed. "I do not believe it! If he has had an accident, where is he?"

Selma hesitated, and Captain Seymour said:

"If there is anything secret about it, I can assure you that we are to be trusted."

He turned to Graves and said:

"Is that not true, Graves?"

"It is true, Sir," Graves replied, "and I feel sure if Miss Linton allows it, His Grace would like to see you."

"Allows it!" Lady Bramwell exclaimed, turning back. "What do you mean, allows it?"

"His Grace had a fall and was very badly concussed, M'Lady. He has been allowed no visitors for over a week," Graves replied.

"Then he will be very glad to see us," Lady Bramwell said, "and I insist that we are taken to see him immediately."

She spoke so positively that she made Selma feel insignificant and helpless.

She also had the feeling that perhaps the Duke would be very pleased to see his friends.

She thought that the reason for his being so disagreeable this morning was not only that he was feeling ill but that he was bored.

Selma was very conscious that he resented being confined to his bed.

She thought also that he must feel it constricting to be in such a small room, when the huge, magnificent apartments in his own house were waiting for him.

She made up her mind and said:

"My horse is outside and, if you will follow me, I will take you to where His Grace is staying."

Lady Bramwell looked at Charles and raised her eyebrows in a supercilious manner.

*　　*　　*

Selma went down the steps and the groom helped her into the saddle.

As usual, she had come up to Mortlyn in her ordinary cotton dress and had not remembered to wear a bonnet.

She looked lovely, but it was fortunate that she did

not hear Doreen Bramwell say as she seated herself in her luxurious carriage:

"Really, Charles, I have no idea who this strange and impertinent young woman can be. Judging by her clothes, she is certainly of no consequence."

"She said she was nursing Wade," Charles Seymour replied.

"'Nursing' is certainly a new word for what I suspect," Lady Bramwell retorted. "I should have thought that Wade would have more sense than to bring a woman of that sort into his own home."

Charles Seymour stretched out his legs.

"You are jumping to conclusions, Doreen, which I am quite sure are incorrect."

"Then kindly explain to me why that young woman is giving herself 'airs,' and why Wade is not at home."

"I expect there is a good explanation," Charles Seymour answered, although he admitted to himself that it did seem a little odd.

Selma led them through the Park to the Dovecote.

Only when she reached the drive did she hurry Rufus ahead.

She dismounted at the front-door and called out to one of the gardeners working at the front of the house to take Rufus to the stables.

She then ran up the stairs.

The Duke was sitting at the window in the sunshine and was reading a newspaper as she came into the room.

"Oh, there you are!" he exclaimed. "I have been asking for you for some time and I am feeling very neglected."

"I am sorry," Selma said, walking towards him. "I had to go and bandage Oliver's leg."

She paused and then added:

"And, if you remember, you told me to leave you alone."

"I did not mean that literally," the Duke replied.

"There is no need for you to be alone at the moment," Selma said, "because some friends have arrived to see you."

"Friends?" the Duke questioned.

"Captain Charles Seymour, who says he is a great friend of yours, and Lady Bramwell."

To Selma's surprise, the Duke did not look as pleased as she expected.

He gave an exclamation and there was a frown between his eyes.

"I am ... sorry," she said quickly, "very sorry if I have done anything ... wrong in ... bringing them ... here."

She hesitated.

"They have come ... all the way from ... London to ... see you, and I thought they would ... prevent you from ... feeling so ... bored."

"Who said I was bored?" the Duke demanded.

"You did when you were being cross this morning."

There was silence and then the Duke said:

"As they are here, I suppose I shall have to see them. But I thought you insisted that I was kept quiet."

"What I really ... wanted was for ... you to be ... happy," Selma answered.

She spoke as she was already walking back towards the door, and she thought it unlikely that he had heard her.

*   *   *

She ran down the stairs to find the two people from London talking to Mr. Watson.

There was an expression of relief on his face when he saw her.

As she reached the Hall, Selma spoke to Charles Seymour, feeling too intimidated by Lady Bramwell to address her.

"His Grace is delighted to see you," she said. "At the same time, please do not stay too long. He had a very bad headache last night."

"I understand," Charles Seymour replied. "You had better come and tell us when our time is up."

Lady Bramwell, however, did not speak.

She merely swept towards the stairs with a rustle of her silk gown and deliberately, Selma thought, averted her eyes so as not to look at her.

Because she felt frightened of doing the wrong thing, she said to Mr. Watson:

"Will you please take His Grace's guests upstairs?"

Without waiting for his reply, Selma moved away quickly into the Drawing Room.

* * *

The room was full of sunshine and the fragrance of flowers, and Selma felt as if, in some way, it comforted and soothed her.

It swept away the agitation she had felt because of Lady Bramwell's hostility.

She went to the window to look out at the Rose Garden.

She felt that the beauty of it was something which could not be hurt or spoiled.

Then she knew that the happiness that she had known in the last few days through looking after the Duke was over.

She had been able to see, to hear, and to listen to him. Now his own world was changing him again.

When he left, there would be only the Herb Garden by which to remember him.

There was a feeling in her breast as if there were a hard stone there instead of her heart.

She went out of the house and hurried to the Herb Garden as a child might seek its mother's protection.

* * *

The fountain was playing and Selma thought that the birds were singing more beautifully than in any other part of the garden.

As she sat down on the carved stone seat which stood against one of the walls, Selma told herself to count her blessings and realise how fortunate she was.

Not only had she been allowed to live in one of the most beautiful little houses she could imagine, but she had also been there with the man she loved.

She knew that after today, if she never saw him again, she would always feel that part of him still remained in the house and belonged exclusively to her.

Then she thought of the beautiful face of Lady Bramwell and tried to laugh at herself.

"I am jealous," she told herself frankly. "How could anything be more ridiculous than for someone as insignificant as myself to love the Duke?"

She thought it was like looking at the moon and wishing for the impossible.

At least for a short while she had been necessary to him.

*　　*　　*

If she heard the conversation which was taking place in the Duke's room, she would not have been surprised.

"Dearest Wade," Doreen Bramwell was saying in a soft, beguiling voice, "how could you be so cruel and so unkind as not to let us know that you were ill?"

She paused for him to answer, and when he was silent, went on:

"If you had sent word to London, I, at any rate, would have come down immediately."

"I was not in a condition to send for anyone," the Duke replied. "I was thrown over my horse's head and very nearly broke my neck."

Doreen Bramwell gave a cry of horror.

It was an affected sound, the Duke thought, and was as over-dramatic as the way she clasped her hands together and looked at him with what she believed was a stricken expression.

"How could such a thing have happened to you?" she asked. "You, of all people, who are the finest and most magnificent rider there has ever been!"

The Duke did not reply and, after a moment, Charles Seymour said:

"What happened, Wade? It is certainly unusual for you to take a fall."

"I will tell you about it another time," the Duke replied evasively.

"What I do not understand," Doreen Bramwell intervened, "is why you are here. Why not at Mortlyn?"

"It was the nearest house to where I was injured," the Duke said briefly.

"Does it belong to that strange girl who told us that she was nursing not only you, but also your nephew, Oliver?"

"I was surprised to hear that Oliver is laid up," Charles said before the Duke could reply.

"He narrowly escaped being killed," the Duke replied, "when a statue fell from the roof and smashed against his leg."

Charles Seymour looked at the Duke in astonishment.

"Surely that was an extraordinary thing to happen at Mortlyn?" he questioned. "I thought you were so particular about the statues being secure because they were so valuable."

"I am."

The eyes of the two men met.

Charles was aware that it was something that the Duke did not want to talk about while Doreen Bramwell was there.

"I suppose we may stay for luncheon," he asked. "In which case, I am sure Doreen would like to tidy herself."

"Yes, of course," the Duke said absent-mindedly, as if he were thinking of something else.

He rang the bell by his side and instantly, which told him that Daws had been hovering outside, the door opened:

"Your Grace rang?"

"Yes, Daws. Lady Bramwell would like to tidy herself and both Her Ladyship and Captain Seymour will be staying for luncheon."

"I'll inform Chef, Your Grace," Daws replied, and bowed to Lady Bramwell, saying:

"If Her Ladyship will come this way?"

He waited as Doreen Bramwell rose gracefully to her feet.

She stood for a moment beside the Duke's chair before she put her hand over his, saying:

"I am so very, very worried about you, dearest Wade."

He did not reply and, after a second, she moved towards the door, walking with a contrived elegance which had always evoked high regard from her admirers.

As the door closed behind her, Charles sat down again and asked:

"What the hell is going on? What has happened to you?"

"Giles," the Duke replied.

"I wondered if it was something like that."

"He damn nearly killed me and would have done had it not been for Selma Linton."

"Tell me everything," Charles pleaded.

The Duke told him what had happened to Oliver and how he himself had been thrown from his horse and would have been bludgeoned to death if Selma had not saved him.

"By God, that girl has got pluck!" Charles ejaculated. "The whole thing sounds to me like something out of a novelette."

"That is what I thought myself," the Duke agreed, "but I assure you it was a painful experience which I hope will not occur again."

"What are you going to do about Giles?"

The Duke shrugged his shoulders.

"But Wade, you cannot stay here indefinitely—guarded by day and night. If you come back to London . . ."

"Giles will be waiting," the Duke finished. "You know as well as I do there is nothing I can do about it."

Charles put his hand up to his forehead.

"I can hardly believe that what you are telling me is true," he said. "Surely Giles can be arrested on some charge or other?"

"You think of one."

Charles did not answer, and the Duke went on:

"Nobody could identify him as being the man who pushed the statue off the roof."

He paused, then continued:

"The men who caused my fall were, according to Selma, rough Cockneys, and even she could not identify them again. Anyhow, Giles would naturally disown them."

"It is the most ghastly conundrum I have ever listened to," Charles said. "You know, Wade, that I am prepared to help protect you if you want me."

"Of course I want you," the Duke said, "but not Doreen Bramwell."

Charles Seymour looked surprised.

"From what she told me . . ." he began.

The Duke was about to say something, when the subject of their conversation came back into the room.

She had removed her bonnet and her travelling-cloak and was well aware that she looked exquisitely beautiful and that it would be difficult for any man not to find her alluring.

She moved towards the Duke to take his hand once again in both of hers.

"I have been thinking, dearest Wade," she said, "that

you must somehow come back to London immediately. Then you could have the finest Physicians available to examine you."

She paused and then continued:

"I am sure that it will be only a very short time before you will be yourself again."

"I am already much better," the Duke said.

"That is not enough for me," she replied. "I have no faith in these country 'quacks' who, the maids have been telling me, have been treating you with herbs."

She gave a little laugh as she said:

"All that is so old-fashioned today, when we have real Physicians, and who better than those who attend on the dear Queen?"

She pressed the Duke's hand as she said:

"I will send for the most eminent of them the moment you return to Mortlyn House."

The Duke had been listening to what she had been saying with a mocking expression on his face and a twist to his lips.

Then, as Charles was expecting him to say something scathing, Daws announced:

"Luncheon is ready, Your Grace, for Her Ladyship and Captain Seymour."

"It is so sad," Doreen Bramwell said, "that you cannot have luncheon with us, but we shall hurry back to you, dearest, as soon as we have finished."

She paused and then added:

"I think it would be wise if Charles allowed me to speak to you alone, because having so many people in the room is bad for you."

The Duke gave his friend Charles a look which should have told him it was the last thing he wanted.

Unfortunately, he was not paying attention, and, with Lady Bramwell still gushing over the Duke and promising to hurry their luncheon, they left the room.

As soon as the Duke guessed they would have reached the Dining Room, he rang his bell.

Daws came hurrying in carrying a tray, which he set down on a table in front of the Duke.

"Here is your luncheon, Your Grace," he said. "Mind you, eat it while it is hot."

"I rang because I wanted to see Miss Selma," the Duke replied. "Unless, of course, she is having luncheon in the Dining Room."

He knew perceptively, however, that this was something which Selma would not do, and Daws said:

"I think, Your Grace, that Miss Selma is in the Herb Garden."

"Then fetch her," the Duke ordered.

"It would be best to wait until I have served you with the next course, Your Grace."

"Fetch her," the Duke ordered again.

Daws, realising there was no point in arguing with his Master, hurried down the stairs.

He told the Footman in the Hall to collect the Duke's food from the Kitchen and then went out across the garden.

He had seen Selma going there soon after Lady Bramwell arrived.

Because there was nothing that went on in London or at Mortlyn of which Daws was not aware, he was sure that Lady Bramwell had made herself unpleasant in a way which Selma would not understand.

"She'll be no match," Daws told himself, "for them prowling leopardesses like Her Ladyship."

*   *   *

Daws reached the Herb Garden and found Selma sitting on the seat watching the fountain.

He was at her side before she realised he was there.

"His Grace wants you," he said briefly.

Selma sprang to her feet.

"He is not in pain?"

It was the first thought which came into her head, and her anxiety was very apparent.

"No, His Grace is all right," Daws said. "He asked for you and wouldn't even let me bring up his next course before I fetched you."

Selma gave him a quick glance.

"There is nothing wrong, is there?"

"I don't know, Miss, and that's the truth," Daws answered. "But I wouldn't be surprised."

Selma hurried back to the house anxiously wondering why the Duke wanted her.

* * *

As she reached his bedroom, Selma found the Footman taking away what Daws called "the second course" and realised that it was untouched.

She went into the bedroom.

As she walked towards him, the Duke was watching her.

"You promised me," she said as she reached him, "that you would try to eat sensibly. You have got to build up your strength."

"I am not hungry," the Duke said. "But I cannot imagine, Selma, why you allowed me to have visitors."

He paused and then went on:

"I am not feeling strong enough for all this chatter."

Selma drew in her breath.

"I am sorry," she said humbly. "I thought you would be so glad to see your friends."

"I intend to send them back to London after they have had luncheon."

He paused briefly and then continued:

"If they question you, you must make it quite clear that I am not strong enough to have people talking to me. It might even be dangerous, considering my head was injured."

"I will do my best to make them realise that," Selma replied.

At the same time, her heart was singing.

However beautiful Lady Bramwell was, the Duke did not want her.

Suddenly the sunshine was more golden and the birds seemed to be singing more loudly. The fragrance of the flowers was stronger than it had been before.

She wondered what the Duke would say if she told him how happy he had made her.

She had no idea that there was a radiance about her that made her look quite different from when she had first come into the room.

* * *

The Duke had not considered that Doreen Bramwell would refuse to do what he wished.

She and Charles Seymour had come upstairs after the Chef's considerable ingenuity in contriving to produce an excellent luncheon at short notice.

She said as she entered the Duke's room:

"Now I am going to send Charles into the garden while I talk to you, dearest Wade."

"I have already decided," the Duke replied, "that Charles should take you back to London as soon as possible."

He paused and then added:

"I am sorry to appear inhospitable, but already my head is beginning to pain me and I usually lie down after luncheon."

"I understand," Doreen said in a soft voice. "I promise not to keep you long, but I have something to tell you."

She gave him a meaningful glance as she spoke, which he did not understand.

There was nothing which Charles Seymour could do except to say:

"I will order the carriage to be brought round at half past two."

He walked from the room and went in search of Selma.

He was deeply intrigued as to who this lovely and exceedingly unusual-looking girl could be.

He wanted to know why she rather than one of the enormous staff at Mortlyn was attending to the Duke.

* * *

Selma had left the Duke when she reckoned that luncheon in the Dining Room would soon be finished.

She knew then that Lady Bramwell and Captain Seymour would come upstairs.

She was not hungry, and she was sure that Nanny would have kept her something to eat.

In the meantime she went into the Drawing Room and started to arrange some flowers which had been brought in earlier by one of the gardeners.

Although the Duke had not yet come downstairs, Selma was determined that when he did so, he would find every room in the house looking beautiful.

Perhaps that would make him less likely to feel that she was an interloper and to resent her presence in what was a family residence.

She had always had a skill with flowers which made them look as lovely in the house as when they were growing outside.

Because she was doing them to please the Duke, she took even more pains than usual in filling first the Wedgwood bowls which had been the delight of her mother.

Then she had cleaned the bowls of cut glass until they shone like diamonds.

Selma was arranging some pink moss roses in one,

when Charles Seymour came into the room.

She looked up at him a little apprehensively.

He said as he walked towards her:

"Please do not stop what you are doing. I want to talk to you about the Duke and to ask you what we can do about Giles Lyne."

"He has told you what actually happened?" Selma asked.

"Wade is my oldest friend," Charles answered. "We have few secrets from each other. We were at Eton and Oxford together and we served in the same Regiment."

He paused and then continued:

"It will not surprise you, Miss Linton, to know that I admire him more than any man I have ever met."

"He is . . . wonderful," Selma said.

She looked up at Charles and went on in her soft voice:

"At the same time, how is it possible, even if we surround him with a whole Regiment of soldiers, to prevent him being murdered in some unexpected and horrible manner by his cousin?"

"It is intolerable and very frightening," Charles exclaimed. "We have to do something!"

Selma looked at him helplessly and he said:

"The Duke has not told Lady Bramwell the truth. I shall take her back to London, which is what he wants, but I intend to return immediately."

He paused and then added:

"If I cannot stay with you here, then at least there will be a bed for me at Mortlyn."

Selma laughed.

"My Nurse said this morning that the house was bursting at its seams, and that is actually the truth!"

Then she was serious as she said:

"I am sure, as you know the Duke so well, he would be very glad to have you with him."

She smiled at Charles and went on:

"Those who are guarding him are getting tired of being alert both by day and by night."

She gave a little sigh before she added:

"It is almost . . . worse when . . . nothing happens."

"I know exactly what you mean," Charles said. "Now, tell me about yourself. Why, if you live at Mortlyn, have I never met you before?"

"I am the Vicar's daughter," Selma replied. "At least I was until Papa died a few weeks ago."

"I am sorry."

"I miss him desperately," Selma said. "But at the same time, His Grace has been very kind and allowed me to move into this marvellous house when the Vicarage was wanted by the new incumbent."

"So that is the explanation," Charles said. "I was wondering why I have never been here before."

"It is very beautiful," Selma said.

"And therefore very appropriate for you," he spoke as he would to any other woman of his acquaintance.

Selma looked surprised and he realised she was not used to compliments.

He also realised that, with her unusual and exquisite beauty, she was completely unspoiled and, he thought, until now, undiscovered.

Aloud, he asked:

"Are you really treating the Duke with herbs instead of ordinary medicines?"

"The Herb Garden belonging to this house has been there since the reign of Queen Elizabeth," Selma said.

She paused and then went on:

"My mother taught me the magic of herbs. That is exactly what they are for those who are healed by them."

"You are certainly fortunate in having such a distinguished patient," Charles remarked.

He could not help the touch of sarcasm in his voice.

He was thinking that if Selma wanted a reference for

the future, she had certainly aimed high in treating the Duke of Mortlyn.

She did not reply, and he thought perhaps he had been rude.

Then she said:

"If you could spare a few moments before you return to London . . . it would be very . . . kind if you would . . . talk to Oliver."

She went on to explain:

"There is no room for him to stay here, and he is getting bored and impatient with being alone. What he wants is what my Nanny calls 'company.'"

Charles Seymour laughed.

"I will certainly go and see Oliver and take Lady Bramwell with me."

He paused and then continued:

"I think that we should interrupt the *tête-à-tête* which is taking place upstairs. It has gone on long enough."

He saw Selma look up at the ceiling, almost as if she expected to reach the Duke by disappearing through it.

Then she said in a low voice:

"Perhaps you would be kind enough to tell Lady Bramwell that . . . she should not . . . overtire His Grace."

"I will do as you ask me," Charles Seymour said. "But I have the feeling that I shall not be particularly welcome."

He was, although he was not aware of it, quite wrong in this particular.

* * *

As soon as Doreen Bramwell was alone with the Duke, she had gone down on her knees beside his chair and lifted her lips to his, saying:

"Oh, Wade, darling, you have no idea how I have been longing to see you! How worried I was not to have heard from you!"

117

"There was nothing I could do," the Duke said shortly.

She was close against his chest, but he did not put his arms around her.

As if she were too impatient to wait, she moved herself a little higher so that now her lips were almost on a level with his.

"I have something very wonderful to tell you," she said. "It is, of course, a secret."

"Then perhaps it is a mistake to tell anyone," the Duke said in a dry tone.

"It concerns you and it concerns me, my darling," she said. "I know it will make you very, very happy."

The Duke looked somewhat sceptical, as if he thought that unlikely.

Then, moving her body even nearer to him—if that were possible—she said:

"My husband saw the Royal Physician two days ago and he was told—of course it is horrifying for him—that his heart is in a very bad state and he is likely to die at any moment."

The Duke still did not say anything, and she went on:

"Of course, I am very upset for him. But, as you know, we have been more or less separated—except in public—for years."

Her hand crept up to caress the Duke's face as she whispered:

"Now it is only a question of time, my wonderful, magnificent Wade, before we can be together as we want to be for ever."

The Duke was astonished and seriously startled.

He had never in his wildest imagination thought of marrying Doreen Bramwell.

He had, in fact, decided after that first night of love that she no longer appealed to him.

He had thought that when he told Watson to send the orchids, that was the end of the affair.

It was certainly shorter and quicker than any other of his intrigues.

He could not explain it to himself but, beautiful though she was, Doreen Bramwell no longer attracted him.

Now he realised that what had happened to him before had happened again.

While to him she had been but a passing fancy, she had fallen in love.

He should have known from past experience that this invariably meant tears, recriminations, and the plaintive question. Why did he no longer love her?

He had heard it so often and he knew that with the best will in the world, however beautiful a woman might be, however ardently he pursued her, when she finally surrendered, the magic would evaporate.

He would no longer wish to touch her.

Why this should happen, he had no idea.

He just knew that it did and, when the curtain came down, it was final and nothing he could say or do would make him feel any different.

He had actually thought, when Doreen Bramwell came into his room before luncheon, that her beauty, although it was undeniable, was somehow too conventional for him even to admire it.

Now he could imagine nothing more disastrous to his happiness than that he should have Doreen as his wife.

He was aware that everything about her was contrived and artificial.

"I think, Doreen . . ." he began.

He was trying to find words with which to tell her that she must not anticipate her husband's death.

Then, as though she sensed that he was not as excited as she had expected him to be, Doreen put her arms around his neck to draw his head down to hers.

At the same time, her lips were on his.

Because the movement surprised him and also because she was touching his injury, he gave a sharp cry of protest and pushed her away from him.

119

"My neck!" he exclaimed. "You have hurt me!"

"But, darling, how awful, how terrible of me! How could I have done anything so foolish?" Doreen asked.

She would have kissed him again, but resolutely he put her to one side, saying:

"You have hurt me. Send for Selma Linton. She will know what to do."

"But I will help you," Doreen protested. "Tell me what you want."

The Duke had, however, found the bell which Daws always left within reach.

He rang it violently and, as the door opened, Doreen Bramwell was obliged to get to her feet.

"Fetch Miss Selma," the Duke ordered, "and hurry!"

Daws, who had been outside the door, had a good idea of what was going on and did not waste any time.

He ran downstairs and opened the Drawing Room door, saying dramatically:

"His Grace has been hurt, Miss Selma, and he wants you immediately."

Selma gave a cry and dropped the rose which she was holding in her hand.

Without even looking at Charles, she ran across the room and up the stairs.

* * *

She hurried into the bedroom.

The Duke was lying back in his chair with his eyes closed.

Lady Bramwell was standing over him asking him plaintively, over and over again, how she could help.

Selma did not ask any questions.

She merely put her cool hand on the Duke's forehead and, at the same time, propped up the cushion behind his head.

He did not speak but she had the idea that he was not as bad as he was pretending to be.

Because she guessed it was what he wanted, she said:

"I think you must lie down and Daws will help you into bed."

"I am in . . . pain," the Duke said without opening his eyes.

"I will see to it as soon as you are in bed," Selma said.

Daws, who had been hovering in the doorway, went to the Duke's side.

Selma said to Lady Bramwell:

"Captain Seymour was just coming upstairs to tell you that he wished to leave."

Doreen Bramwell walked with her head high to the door.

Only when they were both out in the passage did she stop and say with a contrived anxiety:

"I am very worried indeed about the dear Duke."

She paused before she continued:

"I am sure you will understand, Miss Linton, when I tell you not only that he is a very dear and close friend of mine but let you into a secret."

She waited as if expecting Selma to speak and, when she did not do so, she went on:

"I know I can trust you not to say anything to anyone, but when it is possible, which it will be in a very short time, the Duke and I are to be married."

There was only a slight pause before Selma replied:

"I must, of course, wish you both the greatest happiness. At the moment, however, His Grace must be kept as quiet as possible."

"I understand that," Lady Bramwell said, "but, at the same time, you can realise my concern."

She paused and then went on:

"I want you to let me know as soon as the Duke is well enough to see me and for me to stay at Mortlyn. Do you promise that you will do that?"

"If it is what His Grace wishes, I will, of course, communicate with you," Selma replied.

"Now, you must help me more than that," Lady Bramwell said almost in a skittish fashion.

She continued:

"You know what men are. He will not wish me to see him until he feels entirely his own self."

She gave a sound which purported to be a sob before she said:

"But love can bear no restrictions and I must come to him as soon as it is possible."

She looked at Selma almost as though she were challenging her to prevent it.

"Now promise that you will let me know. One of the grooms can easily bring a note to me in London. I will give you my address."

She took Selma's silence as an answer in the affirmative and swept downstairs into the Drawing Room, where Charles Seymour was waiting.

*　　*　　*

"Is everything all right?" Charles asked Selma.

"His Grace must lie down and keep absolutely quiet," Selma answered. "I will treat his neck as soon as you have left."

As they spoke, Lady Bramwell was writing something at the Secretaire which stood at one corner of the room.

She put down the pen and, carrying an envelope on which she had written her name and address, she gave it to Selma.

"Now, do not forget what you promised," she admonished her.

"What has she promised?" Charles asked.

"That she will let me know when dear Wade goes back to Mortlyn. That will mean that you and I can come down again and stay there."

She paused and then added:

"There is no room for us here in this little cottage."

She spoke disparagingly and Charles, seeing the expression in Selma's eyes, said:

"I think it is one of the most attractive houses I have ever seen. But you are quite right, Doreen, there is no room for us and the sooner we get back to London, the better."

"I was hoping that we could stay for at least one night," Lady Bramwell said peevishly.

"I think that is impossible anyway when there are two parties taking place this evening at which you should be present."

He paused and added:

"Miss Linton has already said that it would be a mistake for Wade to have any more visitors."

Selma thought he was being very tactful, and she was also grateful that he was determined to take Lady Bramwell away.

She could not imagine what had happened between her and the Duke.

Whatever it had been, it had not been particularly successful since the Duke had no wish for her to stay.

Selma slipped away and was just about to climb the stairs when Charles ran after her.

"I am going away," he said in a low voice, "but I will come back at once and I will not let Lady Bramwell know that I am coming."

Selma nodded. She did not speak because Lady Bramwell had come into the Hall behind him.

Instead, she ran up the stairs, feeling that her depression had vanished.

She was no longer alone and unhappy as she had been in the Herb Garden.

The Duke did not want the beautiful Lady Bramwell to stay, and Captain Seymour was ensuring that she should not do so.

"I love him," she told herself as she walked along the

passage. "I love him and, please God, let him stay a little longer before he goes back to Mortlyn."

She thought perhaps she was being selfish.

But she knew that once he had left the Dovecote she would lose him completely.

If he married Lady Bramwell, she would certainly not be invited to his house.

She would be alone, and she would have lost her heart completely and irrevocably for ever.

chapter six

SELMA, sitting in the Duke's room, was reading aloud to him one of the newspapers and had no idea that he was not listening.

He was, in fact, thinking that the sun on her hair was very lovely and that her voice had a musical, lilting quality he had never heard in any other woman's.

He had, however, developed, although Selma suspected he had exaggerated his symptoms, a bad headache after Lady Bramwell's visit and the next day he had been somewhat lethargic.

She was aware even more so than he was that today he was almost his old self.

After she had finished the Editorial in the *The Times* she looked up to say:

"I have a surprise for you tonight."

"A surprise?" the Duke questioned.

"Yes," she answered. "Captain Seymour and I have planned it together."

"What is happening?"

"We thought you would be well enough to come down to dinner, and Oliver is as thrilled as if he was going to a party in London."

The Duke laughed.

"I think he no longer misses his rowdy friends and his expensive 'Cyprians.'"

He spoke without thinking, then realised he had made a mistake.

"What are 'Cyprians'?" Selma asked.

The Duke thought quickly.

"They are actresses," he said, "and it is a great mistake for someone in Oliver's circumstances to entertain them too lavishly."

"I can understand that," Selma remarked, "and he has told me he is in debt."

Once again the Duke was wondering if Oliver was in love with Selma. They certainly laughed a great deal when they were together.

He now spent every minute he could at the Dovecote but was quite reconciled to being at Mortlyn since Charles had returned.

They rode together on the Duke's magnificent new horses, then came to the Dovecote to tell him what they thought of each one.

The Duke thought now that Selma would make any man an unusual and exceptional wife.

She would certainly prevent Oliver from making a fool of himself as he had done before he came to the country.

Then he knew that as Selma was much cleverer and much better read than Oliver, it would be rather a question of her being bored with Oliver than he being bored with her.

Thinking of her, he shied away from expressing, even to himself, what he was aware was her affection for him.

He was far too experienced not to know when a woman looked at him with love in her eyes.

And yet where Selma was concerned he could not be completely sure that what she felt for him was love.

Her voice had the same rapt expression when she

spoke of the Power which she believed could guide and help her.

He knew that while her eyes looked at him with compassion and a desire to heal, he had seen the same look in them when she was tending an injured bird or a small animal.

To amuse the Duke she had brought to his bedroom some of her patients.

There was a sparrow with an injured wing, a kitten that had been bitten by a dog, and a small dog that had been trampled on by a horse.

She sat on the floor and treated them, wearing the same enveloping apron she had worn when he had first seen her.

He was aware that she gave them not only her skill and the power in which she believed, but also her love.

'If she has any feelings for me as a man,' he pondered, 'she will soon forget once I have gone back to London.'

At the same time, he was curious as to what she really did feel about him.

Except for the expression in her eyes and the note in her voice, she never talked to him in the seductive tones that Lady Bramwell or other ladies of his acquaintance used.

What was more, she never touched him, except when she was massaging his injured neck.

Then he was aware, although she was behind him, that her eyes were closed and she was praying that he would be healed.

'She is certainly unique,' he thought as he had thought a hundred times since he had been brought to the Dovecote.

Now, when she told him as eagerly as a child what was being planned for the evening, he asked:

"Are you looking forward to this unusual entertainment?"

She looked at him a little anxiously.

"You do want to come down to dinner?"

"Yes, of course I do!" he said hastily. "It will certainly be a welcome change from being incarcerated in one room!"

"I know it is very small, and not what you are used to," Selma apologised, "but we dared not take you to Mortlyn in the circumstances."

"I cannot stay here for ever!"

"No, of course, I understand that, but I only wish I knew where Mr. Lyne was, and what he is planning."

"Then you are quite certain that he has not given up, after failing twice, and is still determined to step into my shoes?" the Duke asked.

Selma looked away from him and he had the feeling that she was answering the question with her instinct rather than with her mind.

"I am certain he will . . . try again!" she said at last in a low voice.

"Why should you say that?" the Duke enquired sharply.

"I cannot explain . . . but I can . . . feel it . . . just as I felt when I was going into the wood that you were in danger . . . and knew I had to save you."

She spoke as if her voice came from a far distance, and because the Duke believed her, he tried to fight against his own convictions.

"I am quite certain," he said, "that you have frightened yourself and, of course, me, unnecessarily. Charles has been making enquiries and is sure that Giles has returned to London."

"I hope he is right," Selma said in a whisper.

The Duke knew then that she was still unconvinced and was afraid for him.

*   *   *

Later in the day Charles and Oliver arrived to tell the Duke about the horses they had been riding.

"I shall be riding again in a few days," the Duke said, "so you must both enjoy it while you can choose the best, because that is what I will want myself."

"We are not going to compete," Oliver said, "because as you know, Uncle Wade, you are a much better horseman than anybody else. But Watson said I took the hedge in the paddock as well as you would have done."

"High praise!" The Duke smiled.

"Quite frankly," Oliver went on, "I have never enjoyed myself so much and, if you will allow me, I would love to hunt here in the Autumn."

"It is certainly something we must plan as soon as I am well enough," the Duke agreed.

Selma left them talking and went downstairs to decorate the Dining Room table.

She had persuaded the Head Gardener at Mortlyn to let her have some of his very special orchids, and Graves had brought down the Duke's gold candelabrum.

The Dining Room of the Dovecote was tiny and there was only room at the table for six people to sit round it comfortably.

She had filled the fireplace with flowers and she thought that her father's pictures, while by no means as impressive as those at Mortlyn, looked very beautiful on the panelled walls.

She stood back to look at the table and it struck her that this was not only a celebration for the Duke's coming downstairs, but perhaps also a farewell one.

Now that he was so much better, he would go back to Mortlyn and from there to London, where he would forget her.

The thought of it was agonising, and she suddenly realised that tonight she had nothing special to wear in which he might admire her.

She had never thought about her clothes while she had been so busy nursing him.

She had explained, because she thought he might think it strange, that she did not wear mourning because her father had always disliked seeing women in black.

"Also," she had added a little hesitatingly, "Papa . . . did not believe in . . . death."

"What do you mean by that?" the Duke asked.

"He believed that our bodies were merely discarded like an old suit of clothes and our . . . spirits . . . or what the Church calls our 'souls,' go back to the 'Life Force.'"

"I presume by that," the Duke remarked cynically, "that you expect to be born again, and doubtless as a Queen or a goddess!"

Selma laughed.

"I do not expect anything of the sort! Papa believed that as nothing in nature is wasted, so the qualities we strive for and achieve in this life are used again and again, until we reach . . . perfection."

The Duke did not answer.

He only thought the simple way in which Selma spoke, without any affectation, was very touching.

He realised that any other woman of his acquaintance would have been for ever weeping pathetically at her father's death in order to enlist his sympathy.

Selma spoke as if her father and mother were still with her and he knew that was how she genuinely felt.

Selma, however, had just woken up to the fact that while the Duke would look magnificent in his evening-clothes, and Charles and Oliver very smart in theirs, she had nothing to wear.

She had only the simple muslin gown that Nanny had made for her.

Although it had been copied from "The Lady's Magazine," it would certainly not impress somebody like Lady Bramwell.

She did not want to think about the beautiful woman who had told her that she and the Duke were to be married.

She felt from the moment she arrived that she had

intruded and had disrupted the atmosphere at the Dovecote.

What was more, although Selma hardly admitted it to herself, she had the instinctive feeling that Lady Bramwell was not a good woman.

It was not only because she had been rude and had obviously regarded her personally with contempt.

It was something she knew perceptively, and she did not like to think of her being intimate with the Duke.

Now, because it was his first night downstairs, and perhaps his last at the Dovecote, she wanted to look beautiful for him.

Then she thought hopelessly that there was nothing she could do about it.

All at once she remembered that her mother's gowns, which had been brought with all the other things from the Vicarage, had been taken up to the attic.

A wardrobe had been put there for which there was no room in the Dovecote bedrooms.

She was not very hopeful, but still she climbed the steep wooden stairs to the attic.

Opening the wardrobe, she was immediately conscious of the fragrance of white violets which her mother had always distilled in the Spring.

It brought back her mother so vividly that she felt she was standing beside her and helping her.

"What can I do, Mama?" she asked. "I want him to remember me, and I know how countrified and plain I look besides Ladies like Lady Bramwell."

Almost as if her mother directed her, she took from a far corner of the wardrobe the gown she remembered her mother wearing at a Hunt Ball not long before she died.

She had almost forgotten its existence, but now she could remember her father saying before they left the Vicarage:

"You look very lovely, my darling, and although people will think it strange, I intend to ask you for every dance!"

Her mother had laughed.

"That would certainly give the County something to talk about! Of course you must dance with the Lord Lieutenant's wife, who admires you so excessively that I am very jealous!"

"There is no need for you to be jealous of anybody!" her father answered. "You have always been the most beautiful person I have ever seen!"

"That is the only compliment I want, and one which means more than anything else," her mother said softly.

They had gone off to the Ball laughing and promising Selma that they would tell her all about it in the morning.

She had stood on the steps waving as they drove away.

Then, as she went back into the Vicarage, she had hoped that one day somebody as charming and as good-looking as her father would pay her compliments and love her as he loved her mother.

She took the gown from the wardrobe, realising as she did so that it was not fashionable.

It was a crinoline which had been in vogue until two years ago, when in Paris Frederick Worth had decreed that the crinoline was finished and the bustle was what every woman would be wearing.

It might not be fashionable, but her mother's gown made of row upon row of pink tulle had a tiny waist, an off-the-shoulder *décolletage*, and little puffed sleeves.

It seemed to her like a gown out of a fairy-story.

Because Nanny had always kept her mother's things so beautifully, there was not a crease, nor did the skirt need pressing.

She took it down to her bedroom.

Later, when Daws came in to prepare a bath for the Duke, she went along the passage to look at the gown hanging from the top of the wardrobe in her bedroom.

She was half-afraid that Charles, and perhaps the Duke, would laugh at her.

When she had arranged her hair in what she thought was a fashionable manner, she put on the gown with its big crinoline.

She thought that the Dovecote was the right background for a gown that came from the past.

She felt that anything very new and fashionable would jar on the age-old beauty of the rooms, with their dark beams and diamond-paned windows.

Because she was shy, at the last moment she almost changed back into the gown she had worn every evening since the Duke had stayed at the house.

He had seen it when she came to tend to his neck before he went to sleep.

She had also given him his herbs and, if he had a headache, massaged his forehead.

It seemed quite natural to sit on his bed as she did so and, as he had been aware, she had not at the time thought of him as a man.

He was just somebody who was suffering, as a bird or an animal could suffer.

Now, in her mother's crinoline, which made her look like a rose from the garden, she did not look like a healer, a helper, or a person to whom people turned in trouble.

She looked very young and unsophisticated—a young woman dining with three fashionable Gentlemen.

She had heard the Duke going down the stairs very carefully, being helped by Daws.

She had also heard the carriage arriving from Mortlyn which brought Charles and Oliver.

'I cannot meet them!' she thought in sudden panic, then laughed at herself for being so foolish.

Whatever she wore it would not make them think she was anything but the Vicar's daughter who had been unexpectedly useful to Oliver and the Duke.

Then as she went downstairs she felt as if all the

people who had lived in the Dovecote before her were watching her descent.

The Elizabethans for whom the house had originally been built, the Cavaliers who were said to have been hidden there when Cromwell was "Protector of England."

The families who had welcomed the Restoration of the Monarchy with the return of the "Merrie Monarch" as they called King Charles II.

There had been many owners down the centuries.

Somehow she knew that they welcomed her because she tended the Herb Garden, and understood how important it had been in their lives.

Graves was waiting in the Hall, but before he opened the Drawing Room door for her, he said:

"You're lookin' lovely, Miss, an' that's a fact!"

"Thank you, Graves."

She knew he spoke sincerely, and it made her hold her head high as she walked into the room.

The three Gentlemen were sipping the champagne that Graves had brought from the Big House.

As Selma appeared there was a little silence as she walked towards them.

Charles was first to find his voice and he said:

"Do I need to tell you that you look marvellous and very lovely?"

Selma blushed because she could not help it, and looked at the Duke, as if she wanted his opinion.

He raised his glass.

"To a flower that has just stepped in from the garden!" he said quietly.

He was aware of the sudden radiance his words brought to Selma's face.

"You look jolly smart!" Oliver said, and Charles teased him for not being more poetical.

They were all laughing as they entered the Dining Room.

*   *   *

Afterwards, Selma could remember the evening as the most exciting party she had ever imagined.

Charles and the Duke told stories of their experiences in the Army, but it was difficult to remember anything but their laughter.

The food was delicious, and she felt as if the whole room sparkled like the golden champagne that Graves poured into their glasses.

After the last course Selma knew it was correct to leave the men to their port or brandy. As she left the room Charles said:

"We shall not be long."

She smiled and said in a low voice:

"The Duke must not stay up too late."

"Leave it to me."

She walked down the passage, and as she reached the hall Ted came running in through the front-door.

This surprised her because he normally entered the house through the Kitchen entrance, and as he ran towards her she knew that something was wrong.

"What is it, Ted?"

It flashed through her mind that Rufus had died.

Then Ted answered:

"Oi thinks as Oi ought t'tell ye, Miss Selma, there's bin a strange man round t'back of t'ouse, an' Oi'l thinks as 'ow it's that Mr. Lyne they've all bin a-talkin' 'bout."

"Round the back of the house? Are you sure?"

"Oi sees 'im wi' me own eyes, Miss. 'E were a-putting some'in' on t'wall outside t'Study. Oi sees 'im creep away an' thought Oi'd best come an' tell ye."

"Quite right, Ted! Wait here!"

Selma ran as quickly as she could back to the Dining Room.

She burst in and the Gentlemen looked round in surprise as she said breathlessly:

"Ted says . . . that Mr. Giles . . . has been . . . putting something against the wall . . . outside the . . . S-Study! His Grace's room is . . . directly above it!"

She did not wait to say any more.

Charles and Oliver jumped to their feet, and as they went out into the hall she heard Charles calling for Graves to come and bring young Hunter and the Footmen with him.

She did not go with them but stood looking at the Duke, who had not moved from his place at the top of the table, where he had been sitting at dinner.

Then as he looked towards her she moved hastily to his side.

"He is . . . trying again!" she said in a low voice. "It is . . . what I expected he would do."

"Sit down," the Duke said.

Because she felt too weak to gainsay him, Selma sat down in a chair beside him.

He had a glass of brandy by his side and he passed it towards her, saying:

"Take a sip! You look as if you have had a shock."

"It was a . . . shock," she agreed, "and . . . I am so afraid for you."

She obeyed him by picking up the glass of brandy and as she did so she gave a little cry.

"I have just thought!" she said. "Ted said he was putting . . . something onto . . . the wall. If it is a . . . bomb or something . . . explosive, perhaps you should go down into the cellar."

"I have no intention of moving from where I am now!" the Duke replied.

Selma put her hand on his arm.

"Please," she said, "I . . . I cannot lose you."

He put his hand over hers.

"I am convinced," he said very quietly, "that you have saved me for the third time, and I do not intend to cringe in the cellar for Giles, or for anybody else!"

Because he was touching her, Selma felt a little quiver go through her body.

She thought it was like a shaft of sunlight, or, perhaps, because it was almost a pain, a streak of lightning.

Half a pain and half an ecstasy which she did not understand.

Then as she looked at him with her eyes seeming to fill her whole face, he said:

"I know, because Giles has been foiled once again in his determination to kill me, that I am protected by you, Selma, and by the Power in which you believe."

He spoke so slowly and so positively, without the mocking note in his voice that she had heard so often, that she felt her fear subside.

Instead, her love welled up inside her.

It was with the greatest difficulty that she did not tell him how wonderful he was and how much she loved him.

Instead, she said, and her voice was a little unsteady:

"I will . . . try to be . . . as brave as . . . you."

"That is what you have always been," he said. "You are a very remarkable person, Selma!"

Her eyes closed before his, and seeing she was blushing, he thought this was another thing about her which was unusual.

Every woman he knew in London had forgotten how to blush, and although they pretended to be shy, it was so obviously contrived that it always irritated him.

He thought that Selma in her picture-gown, looking like a rose out of the garden, was just as natural, just as sweet and unspoilt as the roses clustering round the sundial.

Yet even while he admired her, he asked himself what, apart from the danger created by Giles, and the way she had so skilfully healed his neck, had he in common with a girl who had lived in the country all her life.

Her horizons had been bounded by the walls of the Vicarage.

He was afraid of voicing aloud what he was thinking, or that Selma, with her perception, might be aware of it.

He took his hand from hers, and having insisted upon her having another sip of his brandy, drank the rest himself.

Then he rose to his feet.

"I suggest we go into the Drawing Room and find out what has been happening," he said.

"Are you wise? At least now we are at the other end of the house to where Mr. Giles was seen."

"I refuse to be intimidated!" the Duke replied loftily.

There was nothing, therefore, Selma could do but to rise from the chair in which she had been sitting, still feeling as if her legs did not belong to her.

As they walked slowly together she knew that her heart was thumping with fear that the Duke was taking an unnecessary risk.

He might by some treachery on the part of his Cousin be injured again.

They reached the hall, and as they would have turned into the Drawing Room, Charles Seymour and Oliver came running in through the front-door.

"We have found it!" Charles said triumphantly.

"Found what?" the Duke asked.

"Dynamite!" Oliver answered before Charles could speak. "Several sticks of it just below your bedroom window!"

"We were just in time," Charles said, and he was obviously a little breathless. "He had lit it and, of course, run away."

"We stamped out the fuses," Oliver said excitedly, "and have put the dynamite in the fountain!"

"Not in the Herb Garden?" Selma cried.

She could not bear to think of anything so horrible and dangerous spoiling the Herb Garden.

"Graves only put them there while he fetched a bucket. Then he is going to throw them into the lake," Charles explained.

Selma gave a little sigh of relief.

At the same time, she told herself it did not matter what they did with the dynamite as long as it did not go off and kill the Duke.

Graves, Hunter, and the Footmen then came in through the front-door.

"We've searched all round t'house, Sir," he said to Charles.

"You found nothing?"

"Nothin', Sir, an' I thinks ten sticks would-a done all he wanted."

Graves looked at the Duke as he spoke.

Everybody listening knew that the dynamite would have demolished the Study and the room above it in which the Duke was sleeping.

If it had not killed him, it would undoubtedly have injured him.

"I must say 'thank you' to the man who most fortunately saw what was happening," the Duke said.

He walked out through the front-door and Selma knew that he was going to the Herb Garden.

She wanted desperately to go with him.

But she had the feeling that he preferred to thank Ted when he was alone and she felt sure he would reward him for being so vigilant.

She therefore went into the Drawing Room, and as Charles and Oliver followed her, she said as she sat down on the sofa:

"We cannot . . . go on like . . . this! Mr. Giles will . . . try again!"

"I was thinking that last night," Oliver said. "Surely it would be possible to trump up some charge against him? Charles could accuse him perhaps of stealing his pocket-book, or of threatening behaviour with a pistol."

"I thought of that myself," Charles answered, "but I cannot help feeling that unless we can really catch him 'red-handed,' he will escape, and go on trying to kill Wade."

He glanced over his shoulder to see that the Duke had not rejoined them before he said:

"It was a question of seconds tonight. Although actually it would not have killed Wade because he was in the Dining Room, the house would have been irretrievably damaged."

"I cannot . . . bear it!" Selma murmured.

"No one has done more than you have to keep Wade alive," Charles said, "but I think he must go back to Mortlyn. We must have him properly protected, however much it may annoy him."

Selma did not answer.

She was only thinking despairingly that if she were not beside the Duke, day and night, as she had been, she might have no further premonition of danger and would be unable to save him.

They sat up talking about what had happened until it was Daws who put an end to it.

He came into the Drawing Room to say almost aggressively:

"Oi've come to take 'Is Grace to bed. 'E'll be weak as a kitten in t'mornin' if 'e stays up much longer!"

As they all laughed the Duke rose and said:

"It is no use my arguing with Daws when he behaves like a cross between my Nanny, who was very dictatorial, and my Dame at Eton, who was a tyrant!"

While they were laughing, to Selma's surprise he took her hand in his and lifted it to his lips.

"Thank you for a delightful evening," he said. "I am glad that the dramatics came at the end rather than the beginning."

Before she could think of an appropriate reply, he walked across the room to where Daws was waiting.

She thought, although she knew he would not admit it, that he was, in fact, very tired.

"Well, I must say," Oliver remarked, "there is nothing dull or quiet about the country!"

"What is happening now is rather unusual," Selma said.

"I should hope so!" Oliver exclaimed. "First, I miss death by inches, then Uncle Wade is nearly killed in a booby-trap."

He drew in his breath.

"Lastly, the house might have collapsed upon us. I wonder what will happen next!"

"Nothing . . . I pray!" Selma said quickly.

"And so say I!" Charles added. "You are quite right, Oliver. We have to get Giles arrested on some pretext or another. In the meantime, the horses are waiting, and I think we should go back to Mortlyn."

"It certainly has been an unusual party," Oliver said, "but I have enjoyed myself!"

Selma knew this was true, even though the end had been terrifying.

She knew that Oliver was young enough to feel that even the effort on Giles's part to destroy them was exciting.

It was something he would want to relate to his friends when he returned to London.

She knew, however, that would not be very soon for the simple reason that he had changed a great deal since he had been at Mortlyn.

There was nothing dissipated about him now, despite the fact that his leg was still rather tender.

She was aware that the enormous amount of exercise he took with Charles had made him forget the woman the Duke had called a "Cyprian."

She had suspected that Oliver had missed her and dreamt about her when he was first injured.

She thought he was one of the nicest young men she

could ever meet, and she wondered if the Duke had any plans for his future.

He might think it would be a mistake for him to return to London and indulge again in the riotous parties that he had told her about, and drink far more than was good for him.

The trouble, she told herself, was that some young men had not enough to do.

She thought how busy her father had been.

While the Duke and Charles might laugh at her, Oliver should be given some responsibility and duties to perform.

She wondered if she could talk to the Duke about it.

But she was afraid he might think it an impertinence on her part to interfere in the case of someone who was part of his family.

"It is no use my worrying about somebody I may never see again," she told herself.

Yet she had an affection for Oliver and also for Charles, besides loving the Duke more every moment of the days he stayed at the Dovecote.

She had an irresistible impulse to go along to his room now and ask if he would perhaps like his neck massaged before he went to sleep.

It might quite easily be aching from the strain of coming downstairs and also from the shock Giles had caused them.

Then she told herself that if she was really needed, Daws would have fetched her.

She therefore went into her own room and, taking off her gown, hung it up carefully.

Putting on her nightgown, she then knelt beside her bed to pray as she had done ever since she was a child.

She prayed for the Duke's life and that his Cousin Giles would be prevented from hurting him again.

It was something she had added to her prayers from the first moment that she had learned about the statue falling on Oliver.

Now it was something she said a hundred times a day, feeling the only protection the Duke had was from the prayer she sent up to God.

She felt there was no one else to prevent Giles, with his evil plans, from being the victor.

She prayed for the Duke.

Then, not really meaning to but because she could not help herself, she prayed that he would have just a little affection for her so that he would not forget her once he had left Mortlyn.

"I love him, God," she said. "I love him with my whole heart and soul, and if he would sometimes remember me when he is back in London with . . . Lady Bramwell . . . I shall be . . . content."

She knew, even as the words formed in her mind, that this was not true.

If she was honest, she wanted the Duke to love her as she loved him.

But that was impossible—as impossible as flying to the moon, touching the stars, or entering the Gates of Paradise.

He was out of reach, and although she would love him and go on loving him until she died, all she could hope for was that he would remember her sometimes.

It was quite late before Selma fell asleep to dream of the Duke.

* * *

Selma awoke with a start, afraid that something had happened or that the Duke had called out for her.

But as the first light of the dawn came creeping between the sides of the curtains, everything was very quiet.

She knew then that what she had felt was the fear that was always lurking in her heart because she loved him.

She lay thinking about him until the sun rose.

Because she knew it was impossible to go back to sleep, she dressed and went downstairs.

It was too early for the housemaids to have started to appear, and there was only a very sleepy Footman on duty in the Hall.

He had been dozing in the big padded chair which had been brought by Graves from Mortlyn so that he could be what he called "on sentry duty" at night.

He started up guiltily when he saw Selma, but she smiled at him and said:

"It is all right. There is nothing wrong. I woke early and I wanted to be in the garden."

He opened the front door for her and she went out.

Passing through the Rose Garden, she went towards her beloved herbs.

She was half afraid, although it was stupid, that the dynamite might have gone off in the fountain and smashed the Cupid, with his cornucopia, in the beautiful ancient stone basin.

The fountain was throwing the water into the sky, and when she looked into the basin, there was no sign of the sticks of dynamite.

There was only the water-lilies that grew there naturally and were just coming into bud.

She sat down on the seat and thought that the peace of the garden was very comforting.

Almost as if it spoke to her, she remembered how many centuries it had been there, and had seen the good and the bad times come and go.

Inevitably, although it might take time, good always triumphed in the end.

After a while Selma rose and tended to her precious herbs, cutting off any dead leaves.

She picked the herbs that she felt the Duke might want, especially those that would give him energy and prevent him from becoming tired, however much he did.

She walked slowly back to the house.

As she came in through the front-door, to her astonishment she saw the Duke, fully dressed, coming down the stairs.

"You are up!" she exclaimed. "But . . . why?"

"I could not sleep," he answered. "I decided it was time I resumed my usual way of life, and I have always breakfasted early."

"I am sure it is too much for you."

"I refuse to be molly-coddled any longer!" the Duke replied. "Daws is already complaining that I shall have a relapse, so there is no need for you to do so also!"

He spoke aggressively, but Selma laughed.

"As you will obviously do what you want to do, Your Grace, whatever I may say, I will remain silent."

"That is certainly a step in the right direction," the Duke replied, "and I have never liked women who chatter at breakfast."

"Would you prefer to eat alone?" Selma suggested.

"Certainly not!" he replied. "You will breakfast with me, but I will do all the talking."

She laughed again because his eyes were twinkling, and she knew he was teasing her.

She put the herbs she had picked down on the table.

Without giving a thought as to how she looked, she walked with the Duke towards the Dining Room.

Daws had obviously alerted the Kitchen staff, as Graves had not yet arrived from Mortlyn, and one of the Footmen was waiting for them.

The Duke sat, as if by right, at the head of the table, and Selma sat beside him.

As the Footmen brought in the breakfast dishes, she looked at the Duke and thought he looked much better than might have been expected.

He was thinner than he had been before his accident, but it merely seemed to accentuate his good looks.

He no longer had the pallor which had worried her, and his skin was quite normal.

He was looking exceedingly smart.

She thought with a little pang of her heart that now that he was really himself again, he was ready to pick up his life where it had left off.

"I thought today," the Duke began, "that I would drive over to Mortlyn, and I have already told Daws when the servants arrive to send for my Phaeton."

With difficulty Selma bit back the objection that he might not yet be ready to drive.

She knew, because she could read his thoughts, that he was expecting her to say this and to caution him not to over-do things.

She therefore forced herself to say nothing except:

"I am sure you will be . . . delighted to see your . . . horses again."

"I doubt if they have missed me," the Duke replied. "I gather that Charles and Oliver have kept them well-exercised."

"It has made Oliver happy," Selma said, "and I wanted, if you did not think it an impertinence, to talk to you about him."

The Duke raised his eye-brows and she thought he was surprised.

Then as she was feeling for words the Dining Room door was suddenly thrown open and Oliver stood there.

Selma turned her head to look at him, and as she did so, Oliver cried:

"I have killed him! I have killed Giles and he will never threaten you again, Uncle Wade!"

chapter seven

FOR a moment Selma and the Duke seemed turned to stone.

Then as Selma gave a cry of joy, Oliver ran towards her and flung his arms around her, saying again:

"I have killed him, and now we are safe!"

He kissed Selma on the cheek and hugged her and, because she was so relieved and excited, she hugged him back.

The Duke, still not moving, watched them, and as he did so was aware of what he had tried to deny for a long time, that he loved Selma.

He felt the blood throbbing in his temples as he knew he wanted to snatch her out of Oliver's arms, knock his nephew down, and tell Selma that no one should touch her but himself.

Instead, as the two young people disentangled themselves, he was aware that the tears were running down Selma's cheeks.

"What happened?" he asked.

"That is what I came to tell you . . ." Oliver began.

Then Selma, with a little cry, exclaimed:

"You are wet—soaking wet!"

She glanced down at her gown and realised that she,

too, was wet from his riding-jacket, which was soaking, and so were his breeches.

"It does not matter," Oliver said quickly. "What is important is that Giles will never threaten Uncle Wade again!"

The Duke sat down in the chair he had just vacated and filled Selma's cup with coffee as if he realised that she needed it.

Then he filled his own cup also and pushed it towards Oliver.

Oliver took a big gulp of coffee, then said:

"I could not sleep, Uncle Wade, so I got up early and went to the stables and said I would ride Jupiter."

He gave his Uncle a sidelong glance as he did so, and the Duke said:

"I gave instructions that no one was to ride Jupiter except me!"

"I know," Oliver replied, "but I wanted to prove that I was capable of handling such a difficult horse."

"Go on, tell me what happened," Selma interrupted.

She knew that once the men started talking about horses, it would be difficult for them to get to the point.

"Jupiter was playing up a bit," Oliver continued, "but he knew I could control him. I gave him his head as we rode through the Park, and then when I had nearly reached the wood I saw Giles down by the lake."

"What was he doing?" the Duke asked.

"He was just staring at the water, and I am sure he was thinking that if he had not burned you alive last night, he would find some way of drowning you!"

Selma gave a little cry of horror.

Then as if the Duke did not want her to be upset, he put out his hand and laid it over hers.

He felt her fingers quiver and thought it was what he was feeling himself.

But his eyes were on Oliver, who went on:

"Later I found Giles's horse in the wood, but when I

148

saw him he was just standing on the edge of the lake, where it deepens."

"What did you do?" the Duke asked.

"I rode Jupiter straight at him! He did not hear me until I was just behind him. Then, as he turned round, it was too late!"

Oliver drew in his breath as if he were recalling the excitement of it.

"He could not run away as there was nowhere to go, and Jupiter, realising that the lake was in front of him, jumped. One of his front legs must, I think, have struck Giles in the face, for he fell into the water."

Oliver paused as if to see the effect of what he had said on his listeners.

"The next thing I knew was a huge splash as Jupiter and I hit the lake," he said. "I struggled to keep in the saddle and Jupiter started swimming."

The Duke and Selma were listening raptly as Oliver ended on a note of triumph:

"When Jupiter scrambled out on the other side, I looked back, but there was no sign of Giles! I knew then that he had sunk into the reeds which you warned me about when I told you I wanted to swim there."

"There are also shifting sands," the Duke said, "and I have thought for some time it should be cleaned out."

"Do not be in a hurry," Oliver said. "If you ask me, it is a fitting grave for Giles!"

"I . . . I cannot . . . believe it!"

Selma could not repress the sob in her voice, or the fact that once again the tears were running down her cheeks.

She took her hand from the Duke's, and when she searched in vain for a handkerchief, he handed her his clean white linen one.

It smelt of Eau de Cologne, and it made her want to cry even more simply because she was so glad, so grateful that at last he was safe.

"I suppose there is nothing we can do," the Duke said reflectively.

"Nothing," Oliver replied. "Giles is dead, and it is unlikely they will find his body before you have the lake cleaned out, and that might not be for years."

Selma wiped away her last tear before she said:

"You have been wonderful, but you must go to change. If you sit about in those wet clothes, you might be ill again."

"Nonsense!" Oliver replied. "I am as strong as a horse, and that is Jupiter!"

Nevertheless he finished his coffee and got to his feet.

"Can I ask Daws to lend me a shirt and breeches of yours, Uncle Wade?"

"After what you have just told me," the Duke replied, "my whole wardrobe is, of course, at your disposal!"

Oliver laughed.

"Be careful! Your tailor is much more expensive than mine! I am badly in need of a whole lot of fashionable coats and boots!"

"As the saying goes: 'Everything I have is yours!'" the Duke answered.

Oliver was walking towards the door as he added:

"You can tell Charles and Daws what has happened —but nobody else! Let the Village just believe that Giles has given up and disappeared."

His voice was authoritative as he continued:

"After his efforts to blow up the Dovecote last night, he has gone abroad, afraid I will bring a charge against him."

"That is a good idea, Uncle Wade!" Oliver approved. "Let us spread the rumour that the Police are after him and everybody will be quite certain that he will never show his face in Mortlyn again."

He went from the room and Selma looked at the Duke.

"You . . . are . . . safe!"

"And alive!" the Duke answered. "Thanks to you and Oliver!"

"It was very brave of him to do what he did."

The Duke looked at her sharply.

"Are you by any chance falling in love with him?"

Selma laughed.

"No, of course not! You asked me that before, and I can only repeat that I think of Oliver as if he were my brother. That is the way I love him, which is not the sort of love you are talking about."

The Duke rose to his feet.

"I want you to come with me into the Herb Garden."

"But . . . why?"

"I will tell you once we are there."

Selma gave him a radiant little smile.

She had always suspected that the Duke, because he was cynical about her contention that herbs could heal everybody, actually disliked the garden.

Now that he wished to go there, she wondered if she had convinced him that herbs were of service to anyone who needed them.

They went into the Hall and out through the front-door.

There was no sign of Jupiter, and Selma knew that Ted or one of the gardeners would have taken him to the Stables.

She was only surprised that the Duke did not wish to go there first.

They went through the archway in the wall and instantly the fragrance of roses seemed to envelop them.

Without thinking it was a strange thing to do, Selma bent and picked a half-open white rosebud.

"I think," she said, "because we are all so happy that you are safe, that we must celebrate!"

She put the rosebud in the button hole of his jacket and he thought as she did so that she was like a white rose herself, still in bud, not fully a woman, as she would be when she was awakened to love.

He did not say anything as they walked side by side into the Herb Garden.

The fountain was playing and the Duke was aware that Selma responded with her whole being to the beauty of the garden and what to her was the sanctity of it.

To his surprise, he found himself feeling its influence also.

They walked slowly and in silence down the flagged path towards the fountain.

Then the Duke let Selma move in front of him so that once again he could see her silhouetted against the water.

The sunshine was glittering on each falling drop of water and on the gold of her hair.

She looked so lovely with her eyes alight with happiness, her lips parted, and a spiritual radiance about her that he had never found in any other woman.

Almost as if she willed him to do so, he was also vividly aware not only of her but also of the buzz of the bees, the song of the birds, and the fragrance of the herbs.

As if she wanted to know it was real, Selma put out her hand to touch the water.

Then with her hand still wet, she slipped it into the Duke's, saying:

"Because . . . you are safe, I feel all my . . . prayers have been . . . answered, and the fountain is playing a . . . paean of . . . praise and . . . thankfulness to the . . . Heavens."

"I, too, am grateful," the Duke said, "and that is why I wanted you to come here, Selma, to ask you something."

"What is it?" she enquired.

Then as she looked up at him she saw a strange expression on his face she did not recognise.

Instantly, because she was thinking of him, she asked:

"You are . . . all right? Your . . . head is not . . . aching?"

"I have never felt better in my life," the Duke replied, "except for one thing."

"What . . . is . . . that?"

"I am afraid that you will not agree to what I am going to ask you."

"I will agree to . . . anything that you ask me, you know . . . that!"

As she spoke, it flashed through her mind that perhaps he was going to say that after all he did not want her to stay at the Dovecote.

The light faded from her eyes and she looked up at him anxiously as she enquired:

"What . . . do you . . . want me to . . . do?"

"I want," the Duke said quietly, "more than I have ever wanted anything in my whole life, you to be my wife!"

For a moment Selma did not understand, she only stared at him.

Then, as if a rainbow from the fountain and the sunshine became part of her, her eyes were lit with a light that came from the Divine.

As she whispered he could hardly hear what she said.

"W-what . . . are you . . . saying?"

"I am saying, my darling, that I love you!" the Duke answered. "I have loved you for a long time but fought against it because you were so innocent, so young, and so different from anybody I have ever known before."

He put his arm around her and drew her closer to him as he went on:

"I know now that I cannot live without you, and nothing is of any importance except that you should love me."

He felt the softness of Selma's body as she moved closer to him and seemed to melt against him.

"I love . . . you with . . . all my . . . heart!" she said. "You are the most . . . wonderful . . . marvellous man that ever . . . existed! But . . . I do not . . . think I should . . . marry . . . you."

The last words were incoherent, but the Duke understood them.

"Why not?" he asked.

"Because . . . you are so grand . . . so important . . . and I should always be afraid of . . . failing you in some way."

"You will never do that," the Duke said positively, "and I think, my darling, that we shall find that nothing matters except this."

As he spoke, his lips were on hers, and he kissed her demandingly, fiercely, as if he wanted to convince her of his love.

Then when the softness and innocence of her lips told him she had never been kissed before, he kissed her more gently.

As he did so, he knew it was different from any kiss he had ever given or received.

He drew her closer and still closer and told himself he would protect her and look after her for the rest of their lives.

While she needed him as a man, he needed her not only as a woman, but as an inspiration and a spur to his ambitions.

She would be the wife who would revive all his idealism and chivalry which he thought he had forgotten.

As the thought flashed through his mind, at the same time, he was vividly conscious that Selma's body was quivering against his.

He knew that for the first time she was knowing the thrill of being possessed by a kiss, and he felt the same.

She was part of the sunshine, the garden with its healing herbs, the fountain which she thought was carrying up her thanks to God.

He believed in all of it.

154

Just as it was a part of Selma, it was also a part of him.

He raised his head and as she looked up at him she said in a voice that sounded like the music of angels:

"I love . . . you! I love you . . . so much . . . that I am . . . afraid."

"Of me?" he asked.

"That I may . . . lose you, and this is just . . . a dream from . . . which I will . . . wake up."

"We will dream together, my precious," the Duke said, "and nothing shall prevent us from being married as quickly as possible."

"Can we . . . really do . . . that?" Selma asked.

"I have no intention of going back to Mortlyn tomorrow without having you with me," the Duke said. "Now that we have found each other, how could we possibly live in different houses?"

Selma gave a little laugh, and put her head against his shoulder.

"I . . . might have . . . guessed," she teased, "that you would . . . not . . . allow me to have the Dovecote for . . . long."

"It would not matter whether it was the Dovecote or any other house," the Duke said. "You will be with me at Mortlyn and anywhere else I live. I cannot be without you."

"I am dreaming . . . I know I am dreaming!" Selma said. "When I knew that I loved you I . . . thought it was like . . . looking at the moon and that you would . . . never love . . . me."

She gave a little sound that was half a sigh and half a sob as she said:

"I just prayed that you would . . . remember me and have a little . . . just a little . . . affection for me when you had . . . gone away."

The Duke's arms tightened.

"Anywhere I go you will go with me," he said, "and

this is the truth, my darling—I have never ever before felt as I feel now."

"And . . . what do you feel?"

"Wildly in love," the Duke answered, "and so happy that I, too, am afraid it is an illusion."

"You know I will . . . try to make you . . . happy."

"Have you a magic herb for that too?"

"I think it is . . . one called 'Love,'" she answered, "and when two people find it at the . . . same time, they become . . . one complete . . . person."

"That is what we shall be," the Duke said firmly. "And, my precious one, I hope never again to see you looking so worried and so frightened as you have been this last week."

"How could I be . . . anything else when I . . . might have . . . lost you?" Selma asked.

She put out her hand to hold on to him as she said:

"There is no mistake? Your Cousin Giles is really dead . . . and there is no one else to . . . threaten you?"

"There is one way by which we can make certain of that," the Duke replied.

"What is that?"

"That I should have a real heir rather than an Heir Presumptive, although it is doubtful there could be any other relative of mine as despicable as Giles!"

He realised as he finished the sentence that Selma had hidden her face against his neck and he knew she was blushing.

Then he heard her say in a voice that was only a whisper:

"I shall pray . . . every day at the fountain . . . or wherever else I am . . . that I may give . . . you not only one son . . . but several . . . so that you will be . . . safe."

The Duke's arms tightened.

He thought what she had said in so shy and soft a little voice was something he had always wanted to hear, but had not been aware of it.

Now, as he sought her lips, he told himself that he was the luckiest man in the whole world.

Like Selma, he could never be grateful enough for the Power that had brought them together and covered them with its glittering light.

*   *   *

The Duke and Selma returned to the house to find Oliver and Charles sitting in the Drawing Room.

They were talking in excited voices over what had occurred.

As Selma and the Duke entered, they looked up a little guiltily as if they thought their secret might have been over-heard.

Then Charles got to his feet, saying as he did so:

"I can hardly believe, Wade, that all our troubles are over and Giles has at last got his just deserts!"

"I am very grateful," the Duke said, "and I expect Oliver has told you that it must be kept a secret."

"That is sensible," Charles agreed. "We do not want any enquiries as to what has happened."

"Then talk of it only in whispers," the Duke said, "which you were not doing when I came in."

"To hear is to obey!" Charles joked, and saluted him.

"Now I have a suggestion to make," the Duke said.

He walked to stand with his back to the mantelpiece and Selma stood back watching him.

She was thinking that no man could look more handsome, more distinguished, or more attractive.

"I think, Oliver," the Duke began, "it would be a good idea for you to go away for a short period, simply because it would be difficult not to continue talking about Giles, and also you will enjoy the plan I have made for you."

"What plan, Uncle Wade?" Oliver asked.

There was a wary look in his eyes and just a touch of aggression in his voice.

"I thought it might amuse you to go over to Ireland with the Manager of my Racing-Stable. He is a delightful young man and very intelligent. I would like you to help him choose some new horses to start training in the Autumn."

Watching them, Selma saw Oliver's eyes light up with excitement.

"If you find that to your liking," the Duke went on, "I am going to suggest that later on in the year you might visit Syria and choose me some Arab mares."

Oliver gave a little gasp. Then he said:

"This is the most exciting thing I have ever heard, Uncle Wade, and I can hardly believe you mean it."

"I think it would do you good to see a little of the world," the Duke replied, "and also, if you can ride Jupiter, I am prepared to believe you can ride anything, and can be a very good judge of horse-flesh!"

"All I can say is you are a Wizard!" Oliver exclaimed. "Thank you a thousand times!"

He looked over at Selma and said:

"You told me to trust Uncle Wade to come up trumps, and he has!"

"Of course he has!" Selma said in a soft voice.

She was not looking at Oliver as she spoke, but at the Duke, and he was looking at her.

Charles, intercepting their glance, looked from one to the other and said:

"I have a feeling, Wade, you have something else to tell us."

"I was just going to ask you," the Duke replied in a deliberately casual voice, "if you would oblige me by being my 'Best Man'!"

Charles gave a whoop of joy and got to his feet.

"Are you telling me that you are going to marry Selma?"

"She has accepted me!" the Duke said.

"It is the best thing I have ever heard!" Charles cried, shaking the Duke by the hand.

He walked towards Selma and kissed her on both cheeks, saying:

"You are the only person I ever thought could make Wade happy."

"If you are going to be married, that suits me!" Oliver exclaimed. "I was afraid that when I went back to London I would not have the chance to see Selma unless you invited me to stay at Mortlyn."

"Wherever we go," the Duke said, "you will always be welcome. But I warn you, I am a hard task-master, and I shall expect a number of really good horses to show for your labours."

"I only hope you are rich enough to afford them!" Oliver quipped.

Then, as Selma walked towards the Duke and he put his arm around her, Oliver added:

"I am not going to Ireland until I have danced at your wedding!"

"We are going to be married the day after tomorrow," the Duke said, "so you will not leave before that."

"The day after . . . tomorrow?" Selma reiterated.

"I see no reason for waiting any longer," the Duke said, "and I think it would do us both good to get away for a little while. I shall take you first to Paris, where we will buy your trousseau, and after that anywhere in the world you want to go."

She knew as he spoke he was thinking of how she had said she had travelled "in her mind," with her father, and the tears came into her eyes.

They were tears of happiness and she whispered so that only he could hear:

"Now I *am* dreaming!"

Charles then insisted he drink their health in champagne, and the Duke good-humouredly ordered a bottle.

As they were raising their glasses, Daws came into the Drawing Room to say:

"'Scuse me, Your Grace, but as Mr. Oliver's appropriated a great number of Your Grace's clothes, and is askin' for more, Oi thinks I'd better go up to London an' fetch what Your Grace'll be needin'."

"That is a good idea, Daws!" the Duke said. "And bring enough for me to wear at my wedding and take away with me for my honeymoon!"

He was watching his valet as he spoke, thinking that Daws would at least look nonplussed.

Instead, he merely grinned as he said:

"That's jus' wot we expected, Your Grace, an' we've already bin wondering in the Servants' 'All wot we'd give Your Grace as a weddin' present!"

Everybody laughed, then Daws said:

"Congratulations, Your Grace! Miss Linton's jes' the bride I'd 'ave chosen for you meself, if you'd a asked me!"

He glanced at the Duke as if to be assured that he was not annoyed at his impertinence before he continued:

"One thing's certain, an' a good thing, too, we'll all be able to economise in the future on Doctors!"

Then he slipped away quickly in case the Duke should rebuke him.

When he had gone, Charles said:

"Daws is incorrigible! You know, Wade, you could not manage without him!"

"I have no intention of trying," the Duke replied.

"I think he is a marvellous little man," Selma said, "and he bandages far better than I do!"

"You are not to make him more uppish than he is already!" the Duke said.

He looked down at Selma as he asked:

"Do you want me to move to Mortlyn, where I have a lot of arrangements to make for our wedding."

She looked up at him with so much love in her eyes that he thought there would never really be need for words between them.

Then she said softly:

"Stay tonight, and let us entertain Charles and Oliver

to dinner. Tomorrow I shall be very busy, so you can go to Mortlyn, and I will come to you the following morning—if, that is . . . when you . . . want me."

"Why will you be busy?" the Duke asked.

She smiled as if he were being rather stupid.

"I could not go away without leaving plenty of herbs for anybody who may need them!" she said. "I also have a lot of praying to do."

She said the last words so that only the Duke could hear them.

He knew then she would be praying that they would be happy and that she would be a good wife.

Also, he thought, she would pray for sons that would keep him safe from the ambitions of any other Heirs Presumptive.

"Now that is settled," Charles said, "Oliver and I will go back to the stables. We have already planned that this afternoon we will take a lot of your new horses over the jumps."

"If we are not too busy, we will come and watch you," the Duke promised.

The two men left and as the door closed behind them, the Duke put his arms around Selma.

"It has been a long time since I last kissed you," he said.

"Far . . . too long."

She lifted her lips to his in a spontaneous little gesture that he found very alluring.

At the same time, it was so natural, so innocent and attractive that he felt his heart turn over in his breast.

Although he desired Selma because she was so lovely, he touched her with a reverence that was very different from the fiery passion he had known in the past.

Every moment they were together he loved her more.

His whole being was expanding, and in a way growing bigger and finer because of his love.

His kiss was at first very tender.

Then as he felt the fire rising within him he knew that to awaken an answering flame within Selma would be the most exciting experience of his life.

Always before the fire had burned violently, but burnt out just as quickly, so that there was nothing left but ashes.

He knew that what he felt for Selma was so beautiful, so natural, it was like her precious herbs.

There was a holiness that made their love so much a part of God that it would be impossible for it to fade away or die.

"I love you!" he said, and his voice was very deep and moving.

"You must . . . teach me to do . . . what you . . . want as . . . your wife."

The way she spoke made him know that it was worrying her, and he replied:

"All you have to do, my precious, is to give me your heart, as I think you are giving it to me now, and leave the rest to the magic which you understand far better than I do."

"I think, really, that you understand it too," Selma said. "I can feel your vibrations and they are very strong. At the same time, they have a light which comes from the Power that helps me when I am healing somebody."

"That is the light we must both seek," the Duke answered.

His arms tightened as he said:

"Suppose I had never met you? Suppose, when they told me you wanted a house, I had been fool enough to send you away without even seeing you?"

"But you did not," Selma said, "and because you are kind and just, and very, very marvellous, you came to see me."

She paused, her cheek against his.

"I knew even when I was afraid of you . . . that you

were somebody so . . . special it would break my . . .
heart to . . . lose you."

"You will never lose me," the Duke said positively,
"and I will never lose you! You are mine, Selma! Mine
from now until the seas run dry and the moon falls from
the sky."

Selma laughed.

"That is what it had done already, the moon I thought
was out of reach."

He held her closer to him.

Then he was kissing her: kissing her demandingly,
passionately, insistently, as if afraid that after all he
might lose her.

As his lips held her captive and their bodies seemed
to merge into one, Selma knew that her prayers had
been answered.

The love she had found was enveloped by a Divine
Light.

It was theirs now and for all Eternity.

Barbara Cartland, the world's most famous romantic novelist, who is also an historian, playwright, lecturer, political speaker and television personality, has now written over 460 books and sold over 500 million books the world over.

She has also had many historical works published and has written four autobiographies as well as the biographies of her mother and that of her brother, Ronald Cartland, who was the first Member of Parliament to be killed in the last war. This book has a preface by Sir Winston Churchill and has just been republished with an introduction by Sir Arthur Bryant.

Love at the Helm, a novel written with the help and inspiration of the late Admiral of the Fleet, the Earl Mountbatten of Burma, is being sold for the Mountbatten Memorial Trust.

Miss Cartland in 1978 sang an Album of Love Songs with the Royal Philharmonic Orchestra.

In 1976 by writing twenty-one books, she broke the world record and has continued for the following ten years with twenty-four, twenty, twenty-three, twenty-four, twenty-four, twenty-five, twenty-three, twenty-six, twenty-two, and twenty-three. She is in the *Guinness Book of Records* as the best-selling author in the world.

She is unique in that she was one and two in the Dalton List of Best Sellers, and one week had four books in the top twenty.

In private life Barbara Cartland, who is a Dame of the Order of St. John of Jerusalem, Chairman of the St. John Council in Hertfordshire and Deputy President of the St. John Ambulance Brigade, has also fought for better conditions and salaries for Midwives and Nurses.

Barbara Cartland is deeply interested in Vitamin Therapy and is President of the British National Association for Health. Her book *The Magic of Honey* has sold throughout the world and is translated into many languages. Her designs "Decorating with Love" are being sold all over the U.S.A., and the National Home Fashions League named her in 1981, "Woman of Achievement."

In 1984 she received at Kennedy Airport America's Bishop Wright Air Industry Award for her contribution to the development of aviation; in 1931 she and two R.A.F. Officers thought of, and carried, the first aeroplane-towed glider air-mail.

Barbara Cartland's Romances (a book of cartoons) has been published in Great Britain and the U.S.A., as well as a cookery book, *The Romance of Food*, and *Getting Older, Growing Younger*. She has recently written a children's pop-up picture book, entitled *Princess to the Rescue*.

In January 1988 she received "La Médaille de Vermeil de la ville de Paris." This is the highest award to be given in France by the City of Paris.

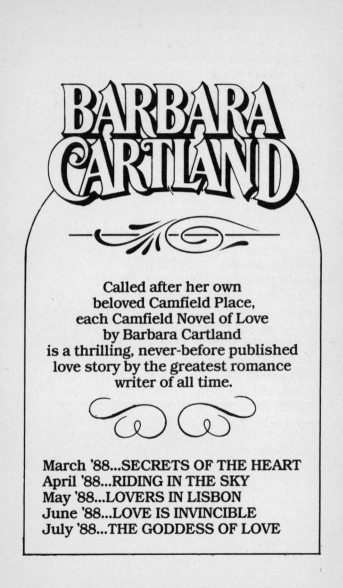

BARBARA CARTLAND

Called after her own
beloved Camfield Place,
each Camfield Novel of Love
by Barbara Cartland
is a thrilling, never-before published
love story by the greatest romance
writer of all time.

March '88...SECRETS OF THE HEART
April '88...RIDING IN THE SKY
May '88...LOVERS IN LISBON
June '88...LOVE IS INVINCIBLE
July '88...THE GODDESS OF LOVE